Once Upon A Christmas

Angie Cottingham

Copyright © 2024 by Angie Cottingham

All rights reserved.

No part of this publication may be reproduced, distributed, or transmitted in any form or by any means, including photocopying, recording, or other electronic or mechanical methods, without the prior written permission of the publisher, except as permitted by U.S. copyright law. For permission requests, contact angie_cottingham_author@outlook.com

The story, all names, characters, and incidents portrayed in this production are fictitious. No identification with actual persons (living or deceased), places, buildings, and products is intended or should be inferred.

No part of this book may be used to create, feed, or refine artificial intelligence models, for any purpose, without written permission from the author.

Content Warning

Before you read any further, please be advised that you are reading at your own risk. There is subject matter in this book that is not intended for those under the age of eighteen. Also, some things could be triggering within these pages. Including, but not limited to, talk of suicide and domestic abuse. You can find a full list of triggers in my Facebook group, Angie's Wonderous Weavers.

Contents

Chapter		1
1.	Ryker	2
2.	Sydney	12
3.	Sydney	22
4.	Sydney	36
5.	Sydney	49
6.	Sydney	60
7.	Ryker	74
8.	Sydney	85
9.	Sydney	100
10.	Sydney	112

11. Sydney	126
12. Sydney	138
13. Sydney	148
14. Ryker	159
15. Ryker	172
16. Sydney	184
Also By	196

"Christmas can't be bought from a store. Maybe Christmas means a little bit more." — Dr. Seuss

Ryker

September

"Man, this beer tastes like piss." I gripe when I take a swig from the bottle.

"Then maybe you should have bought it yourself on the way over," Tom states as he types something on the computer.

"Maybe you should man up and start drinking real beer. Then there wouldn't be a problem. And get the hell out of your mom's basement."

"Apartment. It's an apartment asshole." Tom corrects. "Look who's talking. Why don't you man up and use that talent God gave you and get a real job?"

"I have a real job. Ain't nothing wrong with being a bouncer. Besides, with my background, no one in corporate America will hire me." I remind him.

"You should be able to get your record expunged. Everyone knows it was self-defense."

"Was it, though?" I question.

My sister would be alive today had I not done what I did. But, being a veteran and trained in combat sunk me. Beating the hell out of an abusive asshole is frowned upon when there are other ways to handle the situation.

You should have called the police. That's what the judge said. He should have mentioned they had multiple reports on file that were never followed up on.

"You know it was; anyone in your position would have done the same thing." Tom defends.

"They didn't see it that way. Fuck. My parents didn't even see it that way. According to them, I should have stayed out of it."

Sticking my nose where it didn't belong, as my parents claimed, didn't just land me in jail. It landed me disowned, and my sister died at the age of twenty-three. I should have killed the fucker.

"What are you doing over there anyway?" I ask, curious about what got him so enthralled with his computer screen. It's Friday night, so it's not work-related.

"Mom wants to set me up on a date," Tom tells me.

"Seriously?" I laugh.

"Yeah. Before some annual Christmas party, I've been suckered into going to."

I laugh again. I can just picture the homely girl his mom would find acceptable for her baby. Tom's a great person and he's good-looking guy, but he doesn't know shit about women.

"Anyway, Firefly just released. You know that dating app I did the budget for. I can find a date there to make my mother happy through the holidays." He explains.

"Hmm." I hum. "Maybe. But aren't you afraid of being catfished or some shit?"

"Not really. The guy who built the app runs facial recognition on every member and ensures everyone is legit."

"If you say so," I reply.

"Plus, if I meet someone I like, my best friend can find out anything about anyone." He smiles and winks at me.

"Yeah, yeah. I gotta go to work." I tell him, looking at my watch. "I'll see you Sunday?" I ask.

"Of course. I wouldn't miss the start of the season. Meet me here around three."

I give Tom a salute and haul ass to my car. Hopefully, the traffic is light. Paul will flip out if I'm late again.

Sydney
October

The deadline for submitting my book to the publisher is looming, but I need help to make the words come. Instead, I'm stressing everything else in my life. Mom hasn't stopped bugging me about setting me up with a stranger.

"Syd, please just consider it." She pleads over the phone.

"Mom, no. Please don't try to set me up. I'm fine coming to Nana's party by myself." I whine. Why does everyone in my life think I need a man?

"But honey, Tom is a catch."

"He lives in his mother's basement." I retort.

"Being frugal is not the worst thing in the world, Syd. He doesn't want to buy a home until he has a wife to share it with." Mom argues.

It's a never-ending cycle, this argument. Ever since Gladis introduced her CPA son to my mother, she's been trying to set me up with him. I've turned her down numerous times, but she doesn't want to take no for an answer.

"Just give it some thought, sweetheart. You aren't getting any younger."

"And that's my cue to go. I need to wash my hair." I snark.

"Fine. But Tom is going to be at the party regardless. You may not want to enter this blind, but you can and will at least meet him." She orders in that no-nonsense tone I despise.

"Whatever," I say, hanging up before she can say anything else.

Fuck my life. I'm not interested in meeting this man, but I can research him beforehand. He's on that new dating app, Firefly. According to Mom, he works for the tech company that created it.

I pull up the site on my computer and search for his name. The picture staring back at me is a man with bright brown eyes and eyelashes I regularly pay a pretty penny to have. He's attractive in that all-American way that makes me think he was possibly the star of his hometown football team once upon a time.

Yet, that doesn't at all fit with his profile. He's been a certified public accountant for the last ten years. He likes cats. Yuck. He volunteers to teach math at the youth center and loves children. That part is endearing.

He claims to live with his ailing mother- the liar- to help care for her. Gladis isn't ailing. She's healthier than I am, and I take great pains to keep fit. That woman is only in her early fifties. I'd be shocked if she didn't live another forty or more years.

After reading his entire profile, which is a little on the long side, I decided to take a leap of faith. If I'm forced to spend time with this man regardless of how I feel about it, the least I can do is make it on my terms.

I swipe right to show interest, and the app prompts me to create a profile. I review a list of questions, answering with just a few words. I'm not writing a book here, though I could. I'd call it, "The insane ways we find love."

That's not a bad idea, come to think of it. I pause in my profile creation to write the idea down. I'm sure this will be my next bestseller.

Back on the screen, the app is asking for a picture. Do I put up one of the candid shots from the beach this past summer or one of the more risqué poses from that boudoir shoot two weeks ago?

Risqué it is. I uploaded the photo and clicked submit on my profile. A notification shows that my info is being screened, and my profile will be published in the next twenty-four hours. Then Tom will be notified of my interest. The ball's in his court now, I suppose.

My frustration continues growing to the point that writing is impossible. I can't get my mind to dial in on what I need to be doing. A drink may help.

I grab my phone and call Tina. She picks up on the second ring. "Hey, bitch. Did you change your mind about going out?"

"I really shouldn't. I have a deadline to meet."

"You always have a deadline. Come out with us." Tina begs.

I already know I'm going to go. It's been decided, but Tina doesn't know that. I let her stew and beg for a bit longer before I put us both out of our misery. "Fine. I'll go, but I won't enjoy it."

"I can hear the smile in your voice. You were playing with me the whole time, weren't you?"

"Maybe." I laugh.

"You really are a bitch. See you soon."

Half an hour later, I'm standing in my living area, decked out in a tight pair of blue jeans with strategic rips in the legs and a cropped sweater. I paired a set of black leather, heeled booties with the ensemble. My blonde hair is pulled into a high ponytail with little wisps of hair framing my face.

"Damn, girl!" Tina praises when she walks in. "For a woman that didn't want to go out, you look fucking hot!"

"Thanks," I say with a slight grimace.

"Oh no. What's that look for?"

"Ugg. My mom.."

"Oh, hold that thought. Tell me on the way. Our ride is here." Tina says, dragging me out the door.

During our ride, I tell her everything. I tell her about my mom's fascination with setting me up, about work and my inability to concentrate on the book I need to write, and lastly, I tell her about the dating app. When she is finally done laughing at my expense, she looks at me seriously.

"Your mom is just showing how much she cares. She wants to see her only daughter settled. I wish my mom were like that." She says wistfully. I know she doesn't have the best relationship with her parents.

"You can have my overbearing mother if you want her." I joke.

Tina shakes her head in exasperation. She hates it when I joke about things like that. "Tell me more about the dating app and this guy your mom is dead set on you dating."

I tell her about Tom, or at least what I gleaned from his dating profile. She listens intently to the words before she speaks again.

"He sounds like a catch. And you said he was attractive, right? So what's the problem?"

"I just don't like being blindsided. I don't have room in my life for love."

"I call bullshit. You want the happily ever after that you write about daily. You need to remember that your book boyfriends aren't real." Tina admonishes.

"I don't need a charming prince, Tina. They'd just turn into a pumpkin and disappoint me." I tell her.

"You may need a dork in aluminum foil then." She jokes, bringing a smile to my face.

"I clicked on his profile, FYI. I'm taking this into my own hands. I won't let Mom bombard me with this man at the last minute."

Sydney

Halloween

I don't know what I was thinking with this costume. While I absolutely love it, I regret it as we stand in line outside the club Tina dragged me to. The line is moving slowly due to some stupid kids with fake IDs trying to sneak past the bouncer.

I sigh in relief when the line finally starts moving steadily. "Did I tell you how good you look as a dark angel? That costume is sexy with a capital SEX." Tina tells me as I shiver from the cold.

"Yeah?" I ask. "You're looking amazing too as a sexy little red."

"Maybe I'll find my big bad wolf tonight." She replies, wagging her eyebrows.

I burst out laughing because she looks utterly ridiculous and not all that sexy as she says it. My bestie dances to the beat of her own drum, though; anyone would be lucky to have her, even if she'd only grace their bed for a night.

"How's the book coming?" She asks me, changing the subject.

I fidget from one foot to the other as I talk. Anything to get some heat moving through my half-naked body. "Good. The publisher loved my idea of writing a romantic comedy about the ins and outs of online dating."

"That's amazing!" She exclaims. "Are you still talking to what's his name?"

I can't help but smile. My mother may have been on to something when she offered to set me up. It forced me to put myself out there, and surprisingly, I like Tom. Although we haven't met in person, he seems like an absolute doll.

"Tom? Surprisingly well. We still need to meet physically. He's working on some new project, and it's keeping him extremely busy."

"Does he know who you are?" Tina asks while we step closer to the entrance.

"No. And I plan to tell him when we meet. I still need to find out if he's my type. He's more of a friend if I'm being frank."

Tina doesn't answer, which causes me to look up at her. I find her standing with her eyes focused ahead, drool pooling in the corner of her mouth. I followed her line of sight to see the most beautiful man.

He's gorgeous with his dark blonde hair and emerald green eyes. I look away from his face to take in the rest of him. He's shirtless, with tattoos curling around large biceps and over his shoulder. They continue to his pecs and down to an eight-pack of abs. I think I could probably fit an entire finger in each ridge.

His stomach tapers down to a lean waist and long legs encased in black leather pants. They cling to legs, showcasing muscular thighs. I try not to look at the area between his legs. I'm not at all wondering how that leather encases his dick.

Looking back up, I find his eyes locked on me. Those emerald eyes hold such heat that it warms me from the inside. Sitting on his head is a set of horns that curve upward away from his head. A demon to my angel. He smirks, showing just a hint of fang in his mouth.

Holy shit," Tina whispers.

"Uh-huh," I respond, tongue glued to the roof of my mouth.

"Go lick him." Tina blurts.

I tear my gaze away from the sinful man at the door and look back to my best friend. "What?" I snort.

"Go. Lick. Him." She repeats.

"Why on earth would I do that?" I ask.

"Because if you lick him, he's yours. Haven't you learned anything from those books you read and write?"

"Aren't you the person who told me I needed to remember those books aren't real?" I ask with a shake of my head.

"So pretend you're in one of your books. He's a demon looking to corrupt you, and damn girl, you need to be corrupted."

"Oh my God. Shut up! He'll hear you." I whisper yell.

"Too late." A whiskied voice says, sending shivers down my spine.

My cheeks flame scarlet as I look back at the man. I'm so embarrassed. I cannot believe this is my life right now.

"ID, please." He holds out his hand expectantly. Tina doesn't hesitate to place hers in it. I look at his hand and then back at him—my mind short circuits when he smirks at me again.

I pull my ID from the built-in bra of my costume and hand it to him. He looks down at it briefly and says, "Sydney." He sounds out each syllable, letting my name roll off his tongue.

He hands the ID back to me, and I grab it. He uses the contact to pull me closer, his lips close to my ear and his warm, cinnamon-scented breath wafting over my face.

"You can, you know. Lick me, I mean. But be prepared that if you do, I may lick back. Hell, I might just bite. And angel, I'll devour you whole." He ends his words by nipping my ear lobe, making my breath catch.

Ryker

My eyes follow the gorgeous woman entering the club with her friend. She's sexy as hell in that costume, leaving little to the imagination. It's beautiful on her but would look much better on my bedroom floor.

The outfit is a dark gray translucent material that's sheer except for across her breasts and the valley between her legs. The wings spanning her back cover a delectable ass that peeks between the feathers. Her legs are made longer by the sky-high heels she wears.

Her friend said she needed to be corrupted. I'd gladly take on the task. It was cute watching her face flame. It only heightened her appeal. I don't think she knows just how beautiful she is. I'm shocked when I realize I want to be the one to show her.

The patrons waiting in line make noises of protest at not being allowed entry. I discreetly adjust myself so my stiff dick isn't as noticeable and continue checking IDs in the cold.

After we've reached capacity, a coworker, I don't recall his name, comes and relieves me. He's dressed in one of those union suits that makes him look like a unicorn. He'll spend the rest of the night out here while I spend the remainder inside keeping patrons in line.

I spend the next hour sitting at the corner of the long bar, sipping on a beer as I scout the area for the angel. The dance floor is packed with bodies gyrating together. The bar is also packed, with several lines of people trying to get the bartenders' attention.

Finally, a couple separates on the floor, and I spot Sydney dancing. One man was in front of her, and another pressed to her back. Something uncoils within me as I watch the man's hands move up her sides until they're skating dangerously close to her breasts.

I get the attention of another bouncer and tell him I'm taking a break. He takes my spot when

I stand, which is fine. I won't be needing it for what I have planned.

I go to the dance floor, through the sea of people, and straight up to the handsy guy. All it takes is one look for him and his friend to haul ass in the opposite direction. *Pussies.*

Before Sydney can turn around and see the cause for their hasty retreat, I grab her around the waist and pull her into me. She smells of something forbidden. Apples and spice. *How fitting,* I think to myself

She's no angel after all. She's a temptress, a black widow, and I've just walked into her web. She grinds her ass into my crotch, and I let out a low groan at the delicious feel of it.

I grip her blonde tresses in my fist and pull her hair back. Leaning down, I lick a path from her throat to her ear. "You're intoxicating." I praise.

Sydney tilts her head back to the side in invitation. My eyes on hers, I take the opening and scrape my prosthetic fangs along her skin before biting down. A needy whimper leaves her mouth and reaches my ears.

I move my hand from her waist down to her pussy, cupping it. I can feel her heat and the wetness gathering between her legs. "I want to see your honey glistening on my fingers. Tell me you want that, too."

Sydney looks around and sees that no one is paying us any attention. She looks back up at me and nods. I turn her in my arms until my body blocks the view of everyone around us.

I place my hand back between her legs and move the scrap of material out of the way. My finger enters her, causing her to gasp. I wrap my other arm around her body, holding her close. I work my finger in and out of her. When she whimpers again, I add a second.

I can feel her inner muscles tighten, trying to pull my fingers deeper. Sydney's breathing comes faster and harsher as she gets closer to release. I continue working her up until she grips my shoulders and cries out. She collapses against me as she comes down from the high of orgasm.

She lifts her face and looks at me. Her hair is a little messy from where I gripped it. Her pupils are blown, and she looks radiant.

I remove my fingers and right her clothes. I look her directly in the eyes as I lift my fingers and take in the wetness running down to my palm. When I place them in my mouth and taste Sydney, I groan.

Surrounded by her smell and inundated with her taste, it's euphoria. I smile wide when I look at her again. Her cheeks are pink, and she won't look into my eyes. Her innocence is a significant turn-on.

I look back at her once I've licked all her cream away. "Now that I've tasted you, licked away your essence, does that mean you're mine?"

Her shoulders stiffen, and embarrassment floods her face. "I have to go." She says and rushes away.

I go to follow, but I'm caught up short when a fight breaks out in the corner. I look toward where Sydney ran, then back to the fight.

"Fuck." I seethe as I grab one of the men and pull his arm behind his back, immobilizing him.

I didn't even get her number.

Sydney

N *ovember*

It's been almost a month since my run-in with the bouncer at Dare. I've contemplated going back there several times. I never got his name, and I can't be sure if the encounter was real or if my mind was playing tricks on me.

My core clenched every time I replay that night. His fingers were so thick that the stretch they caused hinged on painful. It was probably fate that I ran away from the scene just as a fight broke out.

As I got lost in the crowd, I saw him looking for me before he thought better of it. My brain knows he's not a guy I'd need to be involved with. He had heartbreaker written all over him, and I had had too much to drink.

It's made for a perfect storyline for a future book, though. My mind is so full of him that I can't even write what I should. Of course, my agent has no problem reminding me of the task.

"Sydney, you've been all over the place lately, and the publisher is getting frustrated with your lack of progress." Claire, the agent says over the phone.

"I know. But it's not like I can stop the voices in my head telling me to write this instead of that. The characters go where they please, and right now, they are screaming for their story to be heard." I explain for the millionth time.

"I get it. I'm on your side here, honey."

"It doesn't feel like it." I gripe.

My call waiting rings, and I see my mother's perfect face on the screen. "I'll have to call you back," I tell her as I hit the transfer call button on my phone.

"Hey, mom," I answer more cheerfully than necessary.

She's still on me about setting me up with Tom. It's been nonstop calls for days reminding me that I need to bring a date to the party that's still a little over a month away. When she's not talking about that, she talks about everything Tom is achieving at work.

As if I don't already know. Of course, I won't tell Mom that. I will not tell her I've been talking to him for a few months and already know everything she's telling me. She already has an overinflated ego.

Nor will I tell her that our banter has gone from safe and somewhat tedious to hot and heavy. She doesn't need to know that some nights, Tom and I sext back and forth until I'm so wet and aching I've resorted to buying a vibrator.

"Any luck finding a date? Or are you finally ready to give in and let me set you up?"

"I could find my own date if I wanted one, Mother," I argue. "I don't know why you're so hellbent on this Tom guy."

"I just want you to be happy."

"Not every woman lives to make a man happy like you, Mom. I like being single." I say harshly.

When Mom stays quiet, I know I've messed up. I shouldn't have accused her of living just for her husband, my stepdad.

"Just forget it, Sydney. I have to go." She hangs up before I can respond.

I sigh heavily. Feeling guilty for talking to my mom like I did, I promise to try. Mom raised me by herself after my dad died. If my bringing a date will make her happy, so be it.

I considered going to Dare and asking the bouncer to be my date but quickly tossed that idea aside. My mom would have a heart attack if I brought the burly, tattooed hottie anywhere near her prim and proper husband. Instead, I open the dating app and send Tom a message. It's time to push a little more for a meeting.

Message sent. I sit back in my chair and let my mind take flight. Emerald-green eyes flash in front of me. I've never let a man touch me like that in public—especially not a stranger.

I blame it on the alcohol, but in truth, it was just him. He made me flustered from the first time I saw him. My brain scattered in the cold wind of the night.

I wanted him, unlike anyone I've ever wanted. When he asked if I belonged to him, I wanted to say yes and let him have his way with me. But I will never belong to anyone. I'm an independent woman. I will not rely on a man.

Like I said, my mom raised me independently, but she had no issues taking from men. After Dad died, she became a completely different person to the mother I knew and loved.

She jumped from man to man until she finally met and married my stepdad. Warren is attractive and filthy rich. He owns an expensive house, several cars, and now my mom.

She's become a trophy wife, doing anything he asks when he asks it. She lost her autonomy. She dresses how he tells her and is friends with only those he approves. And I can't stand him.

I was twenty when they got married. I was away at college and just getting into the author thing. All I knew about the man my mom was marrying was that he was rich and had a son who died tragically.

Mom says she wants me to be happy. That's all I want for her. I wish she'd see that. She claims to be happily married and in love with her husband. I see her keeping up pretenses so she doesn't lose the life Warren's money offers.

I get it. I do. Mom deserves to live comfortably, and if Warren gives her that fine. What I don't get is this need to see me settled down. I'm only twenty-five. I have plenty of time for that if I decide that's what I want.

Right now, though? Yeah, it's not happening. I like my life as it is. I enjoy what I do for a living. I adore creating worlds where the reader can get lost. The best part? No one even knows what they are reading is coming from me. Pen names are fantastic.

My computer dings, letting me know I have a new message. I click to open the messenger on the dating app. I blush when I read Tom's first message.

Hey beautiful. What are you wearing?

Tom looks so straightlaced in his picture, and his profile gives off major mama's boy vibes. Who knew there was this other person behind that screen? It's always the ones you least expect.

Last week, he told me he wanted to tie me to the bed and eat me until I lost my voice from screaming his name. I almost combusted right then. Of course, I asked him what else he'd do, and then I got myself off to his words.

Trying to reconcile this Tom to the man my mother wants to hook me up with is difficult. It also makes me wonder which side of him is the real thing. Is he just kinky behind that keyboard, or is he like that in real life?

Truth be told, it's not Tom's touch I crave. The words are perfect, but I see the bouncer speaking them to me when I get off. I see his green eyes and feel the ghost of his hands on my body. I want more of him. Not this man I've yet to have any in-person contact with.

I'm so fucked. And fucking turned on by the thought of the man that made me come on his fingers in a crowded club. I close my eyes and use voice-to-text to send a response.

"Just getting ready to get a shower, so I'm not wearing anything."

I'm jealous.

"Of my shower?" I ask, laughing lightly.

Yes. I want to be the only thing making you wet.

"Mmm. Yes." I hiss.

Do you like that dirty girl? Tell me what you need.

"I need to come."

Then make it happen. Touch yourself. Imagine it's me. It's not your fingers circling your clit. It's my tongue. It's not a dildo pushing into that pretty pussy. It's my cock. Can you imagine it?

"I can." I breathe heavily.

Good girl. And what am I imagining, beautiful?

"My lips wrapped around your cock, sucking you down my throat," I answer immediately. "I'm so close."

Me too, baby. Come with me, yeah.

I cry out with my orgasm. Holy shit. That was amazing. I swear I come harder and harder every time we play this little game.

Feel better?

"I do."

It's almost Christmas.

"Nice change of subject," I say and watch as the words appear on the screen.

If you could have one wish for Christmas, what would it be?

It takes me no time to answer. "To finally meet in person. For you to do all the things to me you've threatened."

Ryker

That same night across town...

You've got mail!

I laugh when the notification sounds through the room. I find it so hilarious that Tom uses that sound. Technology has advanced so far from when that was the noise people looked forward to hearing.

Tom never claimed to be technologically efficient, though. He gets numbers, not computers. That's my forte. What would he do if he knew I had cloned his laptop? Particularly the dating app he signed up for months ago?

I knew what to do when I saw my angel's picture on his screen one day while we were hanging out. Two minutes of Tom taking a piss and I had complete access to all his stuff. I don't fuck with anything but the app.

I even managed to send him a fake Dear John letter from Sydney. I've been messaging her under the guise of being my best friend. I understand what I'm doing makes me a complete bastard, but I can't help myself.

I've been one hundred percent obsessed with this woman since Halloween. It's got to be fate that she was messaging Tom. However, had I known it was that easy to find her, I'd have signed up on the app myself.

It took me a few days to read all the messages sent back and forth. Ever the workaholic, Tom has made excuse after excuse not to meet the goddess that resides in my thoughts more than she should. It took tons of work to become Tom and then ease into myself.

Sydney is worth it. I know she is. She's also not entirely as innocent as I thought. We've had cybersex a few times, and hot damn, the things I've made her do. She could be pretending, but I don't think so. I could hack her camera and find out, but I feel bad even considering creeping on her.

I stare at the last two messages. "If you could have one wish for Christmas, what would it be?"

To finally meet in person. For you to do all the things to me you've threatened.

Well, call me Santa and sit in my lap. Can I make her wish come true? I want to. But she's expecting Tom—my best friend.

He's the good guy that you take home to meet the parents. He's intelligent, funny, loyal, and he's good-looking. He's also not dated in years. I'm not sure why.

I'm the guy who graduated high school and, to my parents' utter horror, joined the Army. I hadn't been home for six months before I realized what my sister was going through. Seven before I beat her husband so badly he would never walk again. Nine before I was found guilty of assault with a deadly weapon and thrown in jail for five years.

I'd been behind bars when the abusive son of a bitch took a gun and shot my sister in the head and then turned it on himself. At least he spared my niece. All that and my parents disowned me. They told me that even when I got out of jail, I wasn't welcome there.

They blame my sister's death on me. If I hadn't gotten involved, she'd still be alive. I don't blame them for not wanting me around. I know I have her blood on my hands.

The only person that didn't turn against me was Tom. He'd have done the same had he known. Stacey was his sister, too.

I sigh, looking at the calendar. Christmas was Stacey's favorite holiday. Thoughts of her make me think about how loyal Tom has been to me over the years. Again, what should I do about Sydney?

Are you there?

The computerized voice pulls me out of my thoughts. Her Christmas wish is to finally meet. To have me do to her all the things I've been dying to do since that night. If I could wish for one thing for Christmas, it would be her.

Mind made up, I respond, "When?" One word, simple and to the point.

Friday night. The four seasons on the Westside.

I look back at the calendar. Fuck. I have a shift on Friday night.

"How's next Friday? I have a meeting this Friday I can't get out of?"

After a moment, she responds. *Fine. Next Friday. Eight o'clock at the restaurant in the lobby. I'll make a reservation.*

Thinking fast, I type, "No. I want you all to myself. I'll make a reservation for a room. I'll have room service delivered."

Ok...

"Don't worry, baby. I'll take good care of you."

You'd better.

Sydney's name goes dark, indicating that she's logged off the app. I sit there for a few minutes thinking. How am I supposed to pull off this charade?

She may not know now that Tom isn't the one she's been talking to, but she will figure it out when I walk into that hotel room. Tom and I look nothing alike. While he's lost some of his bulk from our days of playing football, I've gained tons. There's little to do in prison but read and spend time working out. I chose to do the latter.

Shit. I didn't think this through very well. I stare at the picture Sydney chose for her profile. It makes me think of her in that costume.

She looks sexy, laying on the bed, back arched and eyes closed as if in pleasure.

I want to make her look like that with me. I want to taste her everywhere and watch her body come alive. I want her to come on my tongue instead of my fingers. I want to feel her clench around my cock.

What I want is to ruin her for anyone else.

Sydney

One week later...

The last week went by in slow motion. I didn't message Tom; I am still determining how to talk to him, knowing what we planned. Would he have changed his mind at the last minute? Would I?

I didn't give myself much time to think about it. I kept busy writing. Even though it was forced, I managed to bang out several chapters in my book, using my conversations with Tom as inspiration. So far, the publisher loves it.

What would Tom think if he knew? Would he be mad or mortified to know his dirty talk was fuel for my imagination? Or would he be proud to be my muse?

Nerves take hold as I enter the hotel. Following Tom's instructions, I walked to the desk and used the name he supplied to check-in. Everything has already been taken care of, so they give me a key and wish me a good evening.

I grab my weekender bag and walk to the elevator the woman pointed out. I use the card to call the elevator. Once I enter and the doors close, I realize this private elevator leads straight to the penthouse suite. I push the button and wait for the elevator to rise.

The ding it makes when it stops makes me jump. The doors open directly into the lavish suite. Across from where I stand is a wall of windows looking out over the city. I'm sure it makes for a beautiful sight when the sun rises in the morning.

The suite is open plan with a fully equipped kitchen. A fully loaded bar sits to the left. Off to the right, I can see a hallway that must lead to the bedroom.

I'm finding it hard to breathe. A drink may help. Thankfully, there's a top-shelf tequila that

I love. I open the bottle, grab a shot glass, and down three shots back to back. I stand there for a minute while my nerves relax slightly.

This is the first time I've done something like this. I'm not a one-night-stand type of girl. I don't do flings. I'm an all-or-nothing girl, and it's been nothing for the past few years.

That is until the bouncer. I know better than to think tonight is all about talking. Tom's last message, which I didn't respond to, made that clear. However, can I do this when my mind is still on the sexy stranger? We're going to find out.

Tina said I needed to be corrupted a little bit. There's no better way to do that than to have a no-strings-attached night with a good-looking, dirty-talking guy. I've decided that during the day, he's sweet, but at night, he's a freak in the sheets.

With liquid courage burning through me, I enter the bedroom. When I get there, I see a folded piece of paper and a long swath of fabric lying on the pillow. I lift them both. The material is black silk and glides through my hands.

I place the fabric back down and unfold the paper.

Undress, but leave on your bra and panties. Wrap the blindfold around your eyes and tie it tight. Lay back on the bed, legs spread, hands holding the railings of the headboard. Don't move a muscle from there. If you do, I'll know, and you'll be punished. See you soon, beautiful.

There's no signature, but it has to be from Tom, right? I follow his instructions and remove my clothes. He said he'd know if I moved. Does that mean he is watching me? The thought of him seeing me right now turns me on. I slow my movements, drawing them out so that if he is watching, he's also getting a show.

Once my clothes are gone, except my lingerie, I kneel on the bed and crawl up to the top. I grab the blindfold and lay on the fluffy pillows. Lifting my head, I tie the blindfold around my head. It's tight enough I can't see but not enough to hurt.

Now blinded, I lay back and stretched my legs out. I lift my hands above my head and feel around until I can wrap my fingers around the metal railing. I wiggle until I'm completely comfortable. Then I bend my knees toward my body and let my legs open. How long will I have to wait like this? I imagine I look ridiculous, and I'm about to close my legs when I hear the door open.

I hold my breath. I see a whole camera crew in my mind, and I'm just waiting for someone to call out, "Gotcha!"

The first touch to my skin makes me jump. I open my mouth to speak, but a hand covers my lips. The hand on my ankle travels north. My skin pimples and a shiver runs down my spine. It's not fear I'm feeling, though my adrenaline is running high. It's excitement.

As the hand reaches the apex of my thighs, it squeezes lightly before moving to cup my most sensitive area. My clit pulses with need, and my chest expands. A small moan rises out of my throat. His hand only remains for a moment before it continues up my stomach to my breasts, which are trapped behind the cups of my bra.

My bra is pulled down in the front. My breasts spill free. Tom grunts as if he likes what he sees. He takes each breast in his hands, weighing them before he grabs a nipple between his fingers and pinches. I cry out at the sensation.

His mouth soon follows. His teeth graze the sensitive nub before he sucks and licks it.

Once satisfied with his attention to my breasts, he starts kissing my sternum and clavicle. He continued until he reached my face. He places a kiss over each eye that's masked by the blindfold. Why won't he just kiss me?

As soon as that thought becomes known, Tom's mouth lands on mine in a searing kiss. He bites down on my lower lip and pulls it into his mouth so he can suck on it. If I didn't know better, I'd say he's trying to leave his mark on me.

He runs his tongue along my lips, asking for permission. I open for him. He tastes of cinnamon. In the back of my mind, something is niggling at me. Like there's something I'm supposed to remember but can't.

He continues kissing me, and I continue letting him. Our bodies aren't touching except where he's nestled between my legs. I can feel the heat of him surrounding me. I can feel him hardening against me. He twists his hips, grinding himself into my pussy.

"Mmm." I moan.

He doesn't say a word. He pulls back from the kiss, and I whimper, already missing his mouth. He kisses back down my body until I can feel his breath between my thighs. His fingers grab the thin lace of my thong, and he gingerly slides it down my legs.

He places his nose at my slit and inhales. Is he scenting me? I can feel my face flush, but the embarrassment washes away when he flattens his tongue against me. It feels so good. He laps at me until I'm writhing beneath him. His tongue laves all the flesh between my legs but never reaches where I need it.

I groan in frustration, and Tom lets out the first sound I've heard since he entered the room. He lets out a chuckle. I remove my hands from the headboard and grab onto his hair. He stops his ministrations completely and holds my hands. He places them back above my head.

I try to remove them, but he holds me still, "No." He says. The tone of his voice brooks no argument, and I find myself wanting to obey.

Ryker

Sydney is a vision in red lace, but she's so much more out of it. I wasn't meant to talk to her, but I feared she'd figure everything out if I let her touch me too much. I'm not ready for that yet. Not ready at all for her to know that instead of the straight-laced man she thinks she's spending the night with, she's got the man she ran away from.

When she relinquishes control, my heart sings, and my dick stands to full attention. God, I want her with a passion that scares me. I've never been this caught up in a woman before. Not when I was younger and not when I was released from jail. Even after five years of celibacy, I didn't want a woman like this. It's an all-consuming feeling. She takes up all my thoughts.

I lean back down and give her what I know she wants. I latch on to her clit and suck. I use my tongue, flicking back and forth at the same time. I look up to see the expression on her face. I can't see her eyes, but I imagine they're closed in ecstasy, just as I wanted.

Her back arches off the bed as I suck and lick her folds. I thrust a finger into her hot channel, and she comes apart with a scream. I want to hear more of those. I want to listen to my name on her lips.

While she's recovering from the pleasure I just wrought from her body, I stand and remove my clothes. Naked and wanting, I walk back to the side of the bed. I grip her jaw and turn her head toward my hard cock. "Open," I order.

She does as she's told, opening her mouth for me and sticking out her tongue. I take my dick in my hand and pump it a couple of times. I step forward and run the tip along her tongue so she can taste the precum leaking from the slit.

Sydney wraps her lips around me, swirling her tongue around the head before she moves further down. I hold as still as possible, letting her take the lead. She lets my cock fall from her lips to get into a better position. She releases the headboard and turns her body so that her head hangs off the bed slightly.

"Fuck my mouth." She orders huskily.

Who am I to deny her? I move forward again and thrust into her waiting mouth. When I hit the back of her throat, she swallows around me, eliciting a deep growl from my chest. I wanted to take things slow with Sydney tonight. I wanted to show her that I'm not a bad guy, but I can't hold back. I start to fuck her mouth and throat with force.

She takes it all without complaint, without gagging. She's utterly magnificent. Sydney moves her hand and cups my balls as I thrust. She massages them in her tiny fist before running a finger between my ass and dick. I jerk forward involuntarily. If I'm not careful, I'll release down her throat, and I'm determined not to come anywhere but inside her pink pussy.

I force myself away from her hot mouth. I grab her under her arms and lift her. "On your knees," I whisper.

She turns over and faces away from me. She gets on her knees and bends until her chest and face are against the bed, and her ass is in the air. The way the light hits, I can see the proof of her arousal running down her thighs. While I want to lick it all away and keep her taste in my mouth, I can't hold off any longer. I thrust into her to the hilt. Sydney cries out at the intrusion. When she moans, I know her cries weren't in pain.

"Please move," Sydney begs.

I listen and begin to move in earnest. With each thrust of my hips, I can feel my balls slapping against her clit. She feels so good that I want to stay inside her forever. The only problem is that I want to feel her body against mine, consequences be damned.

I pull out and flip her back over. I climb up her body and enter her again. This time, I take it slow, rolling my hips and grinding into her. I'd forgotten about her hands until I feel her fingers grip my shoulders and squeeze.

I've never made love to a woman before, but that's what it feels like we're doing. Sydney's hands run over my shoulders, up and down my back, and to my ass. I move to my knees, sit back on my feet, and take her with me so she's straddling my thighs.

I hold her tight against me while I continue to love her. She's clenching around me so tightly that I know she's getting close. I take one hand and reach down between us, finding her clit with my fingers. I rub circles around her in time with my thrusts.

"Oh, God," She cries as she comes.

I keep moving fucking her through her orgasm, trying to bring her to another one. This time, I want to finish with her. Sydney is clawing at my back now. While her nails sting my flesh, I don't care. I love that she's marking me in some way.

My thrusts become stilted, my balls drawing up. I'm so close. "Come with me, baby," I whisper.

"I can't come again." She argues.

"Yes, you can. Just one more."

"Nnngh." She mumbles incoherently.

I don't know what possesses me, but I want to look into her eyes as she comes apart. I grab the blindfold and remove it from around her face.

Her eyes pop open and widen when she sees me. Her mouth falls open.

"You." She breathes before crashing over the peak again, taking me with her.

I fall to the bed with her beneath me as I try desperately to catch my breath. When my heart finally slows, I look at the beautiful woman in my arms. "Hey, angel."

I expect her to push me away. I'm expecting her to call me a bastard, to tell me to go to hell. I'm even expecting her to accuse me of rape or something. What I'm not expecting is what happens next. It's much worse than anything I thought she'd do or say. She starts to cry.

Sydney

I'm not sure why I'm crying. It just happened. Maybe it's because instead of being pissed that it's the sexy bouncer I'm in bed with - and I should be mad- I'm relieved. I know it's fucked up. I know I should want the man I made plans with here, but I don't.

The stranger gets off me so damn quick. I'm not sure what to make of his behavior. He had to have planned this. Has been watching me all this time? How did he know about Tom? There are so many questions that I'm not sure I want the answers to. There's only one that needs an answer at this very moment.

"What's your name? You got mine at the club, but I never got yours."

"Ryker." He says from across the room as he pulls on a pair of jeans.

The name fits him well. "Have you been stalking me?" I ask.

"I wouldn't call it that." He replies.

"Then how did you know about me being here?"

"Why don't you get dressed, and we'll talk." He says, looking at me. "That is if you want." He says as an afterthought. He seems almost terrified of what I'll do or say.

Should I listen and get dressed so we can have an actual conversation? Do I assume he's some psycho that just fucked me better than any man ever has? I decided on the former. Something in me needs to hear what he has to say. I need to explore this connection between us, at least to an extent.

"Come on, beautiful." Ryker offers his hand for me.

I place mine in his, and he helps me up. "Did you want to shower? Are you hungry?" He questions softly.

"I could eat. The shower can wait."

"Let's order some food, then. I'll pour us both a drink, and we can talk."

I nod as I snatch the robe off the back of the door and wrap it around me. I follow Ryker out to the sitting area. He walks over to the bar, and I gingerly sit on the sofa.

Ryker picks up a tablet on the island, pushes a few buttons, and then comes toward me. He hands me a bottle of water and a tumbler of amber liquid. Scotch maybe.

He sits beside me, making sure to keep some distance between us. My body is screaming for him to come closer. My head doesn't have a clue what it wants.

"Was this some sort of elaborate prank?" I ask, looking him directly in the eyes.

"No." He grunts, sounding thoroughly offended.

I sit there silently, waiting for an explanation. I feel the urge to stand when one doesn't come quickly enough. I begin to pace. What is going on with me?

Just minutes ago, I was relieved this sexy-as-hell man made my body sing. Now, I'm getting angry and frustrated that he's sitting there, not saying anything. I turn to face him. "Talk,"

"When I saw you on Halloween, I was immediately struck by your beauty. I heard you and your friend talking. She's not very quiet, even though you were trying to keep your conversation away from the mass of people in line."

"Oh," I say, mortified.

"Don't look like that. It was adorable. It is cute that your mom cares enough to try and set you up. Anyway, I had every intention of taking you to my bed that night. That is, until you ran away.

So, fast forward a week or so. I was sitting at my buddy's house when his computer dinged. Imagine my surprise when my angel pops up on his screen." He explains.

"You catfished me." I accuse. "All those conversations; that was you?"

"Not at first. You did talk to Tom a lot. He kept brushing you off, not making a date. I don't know what possessed me. I know it was untruthful, but I had to talk to you again, and I didn't think a woman like you would talk to a man like me."

I snort. "I let you finger me in the middle of a crowded club. You think I wouldn't have talked to you?"

"You ran away, and you never came back to the club. All I had was your name. Then I saw your picture on Tom's dating app, and now here we are."

"Does Tom know you're here, using his dating profile to meet me?"

Ryker shakes his head. "I may have locked him out of his profile and taken it over." He says sheepishly.

How does one do that? A knock on the door ends our conversation. Ryker answers, and a waiter rolls in a cart of domed plates. Ryker gives the guy a hundred-dollar bill and sends him on his way.

How much does a bouncer make that he can book this elaborate suite, order what looks like the entire room service menu, and give the kid a hundred-dollar tip?

When Ryker removes the domes, the smell of fresh rolls and meat hits my nostrils. My stomach rumbles loudly.

"Let's eat while we talk."

I grab a plate of roast chicken and one of those fantastic-smelling dinner rolls. The first bite makes me groan in delight. Ryker looks at me like I'm one of the dishes on the menu.

"If you keep making those noises, we won't be talking anymore."

I clench my legs together, trying to stop the ache that's starting up between my thighs. Ryker rises from his seat and then kneels between my legs. He grabs my legs and spreads them.

"What are you doing?" I ask breathlessly.

"You eat your dinner while I eat you." He says, a wolfish smile on his lips.

Ryker

The taste of this woman may be my absolute favorite flavor of all time. I know Sydney still has questions. I'm still determining how I'll answer them, but I will. Right now, though, I need to be between her creamy thighs.

I want to hear her groan for me again. I need to listen to her call out my name. I'm done for when her hands leave her plate and bury themselves in my hair. I lift her from her seat and lay her on the floor.

I unwrap her from the plush robe she put on and move back in. I undo my jeans and pull my rock-hard dick from my pants. I work myself with my hand while I work her with my mouth.

Sydney cries out, still sensitive from earlier. I love how receptive she is. I have no patience left. I lift her hips and line my cock up at her entrance.

I thrust into her hard. I don't give her time to adjust before repeatedly pushing in and out of her. I look down and watch as my cock disappears within the hot confines of her pussy.

Seeing her suck me in over and over is the most exotic thing I've ever seen. "God, baby. You take me so good."

"Yes. Oh. Please." Sydney cries.

"Please what? Tell me what you need."

"I need to come."

"Tell me who's fucking you. Call out my name as you come apart." I order.

"Oh fuck. Ryker!" She screams.

The sound of her cries pulls my orgasm from me. I slump over, trying to keep my weight off her. Sydney's chest shakes, and I think maybe she's crying again. I don't know that I could handle more of her tears.

When I lift myself, she's laughing. "The food." She gasps.

I look over my shoulder. The plates I ordered are all strewn across the floor. Nothing was saved. I can't help but laugh along.

"I'll order more if you're still hungry," I offer.

"No." She says, shaking her head. "I think I need that shower."

I carry her to the shower. Once the water is heated, I begin to wash her body. When we're done, I wrap myself and her in towels and carry her to the bed.

Sydney's blonde hair fans out on the pillows, looking like a halo. She's not the dark angel she portrayed on Halloween. She's just an angel.

The kind that shines through the night like a beacon.

I climb into bed with Sydney's back pressed to my chest. Our bodies align perfectly. Having her here like this is the closest I may ever get to Heaven.

"So, why Tom?" I ask the question that's been at the forefront of my mind. He and I are entirely different; if she's attracted to me, she wouldn't be tempted by him.

"You heard me and Tina talking?" She asks. "Well, he's the man my mother wants to set me up with. Since it's tough to tell her no, he will be at the Christmas party anyway; I thought I'd research him."

"And the dating app?"

"Mm. Tom's mother is very proud of her son. She bragged to my mom, who then mentioned it to me. I thought it was the perfect opportunity to get to know him outside our parent's influence."

I took in what she was saying, and I saw their messages. Tom didn't give her half of his true self during those conversations. He's more than what he portrayed.

"Tom is my best friend. We've known each other since high school. He's funny, smart, and loyal to a fault. I know he held himself back during those nights when you two talked." I find myself saying.

"Are you trying to make me consider him a potential date or boyfriend?" She asks me curiously.

"No. It's not that. You deserve the truth. And I may feel a bit guilty for hijacking Tom's dating profile."

"I don't. Feel guilty that is. If I'm being honest, I'm glad it was you. I was relieved when the blindfold was removed, and you were there."

"I hadn't stopped thinking about you. I wanted to see if what I felt at the club was real."

"Me too." She whispers. "I almost returned so many nights, but I was afraid to find out it was some sort of dream."

We spend the next several hours talking about ourselves. Sydney tells me she's an author and discusses the book she's working on. I tell her about serving in the army. I tell her everything except the most important thing.

I don't tell her that I'm the reason two people are dead.

Sydney

One week before Christmas

Getting ready for a party differs from what I want to do right now. I'd much rather stay in bed with Ryker and have a private party here. From the look in his eyes, he'd probably agree.

The last month has been surreal. Ryker and I have spent every spare moment together. A lot of them are in bed together, but most have been spent with him taking me out and us getting to know each other.

He seems genuinely interested when I talk about my mom, but when I broach the subject of his family, he goes quiet. I don't pry, as it's not my business. Everyone has their secrets.

Ryker has spent time with my friends, mainly Tina, and she adores him. One of my secrets is that I do, too. I never thought it would happen, but I'm falling for this man, and it's happening so fast.

I've spoken to Ryker about today, and we decided he would accompany me. He's sitting on the edge of the bed in slacks and a button-down shirt. He looks delicious as the fabric stretches across his large frame.

We also asked Tom to meet at a coffee shop beforehand so we could explain everything to him. Ryker doesn't seem worried, so I let his confidence rub off on me. The last thing I wanted was to hurt anyone, and Tom thinks I just ghosted him.

"Baby, you look stunning." Ryker compliments me as he takes in my red dress.

"Thank you." I blush. "Are you ready to go?"

"I'd rather stay." He says, looking at me lasciviously.

"I wish we could."

He leans in for a kiss, and I turn my head laughing as he pouts. "Come on, Romeo. We're going to be late."

Ryker leads me to his car and opens the door for me. As I slide onto the warm leather, I question where the money to afford something like this came from. The question sits on the tip of my tongue.

At the last minute, I decided against asking. People say ignorance is bliss, and I'm choosing to believe that. I tell myself it's better not to know.

What if he's involved with something illegal? Or could it be something dangerous? Does he sell drugs?

I shake away the thoughts. I can't imagine Ryker being some criminal. He's too sweet, too attentive.

It takes little time to drive to the coffee shop. We park, and Ryker helps me out of the car. He holds my elbow as he leads me down the sidewalk. It snowed last night, so it's a tad slippery.

A little bell chimes when the door opens. We both look around, and I spot Tom seated in the back corner. And he's not alone. Sitting beside him is a gorgeous male. He's what I consider pretty.

Ryker leads me to the table and introduces me to Tom. Tom's eyes are wide as he takes me in.

"I fucking knew something was up when you ghosted me," Tom says.

"Um. Technically, I didn't ghost you. Ryker did." I say, rolling my eyes.

Ryker chuckles, sits me down, and then heads over to order our drinks. When he comes back, we tell Tom everything. Am I crazy, or does Tom look relieved by the news?

The gorgeous man beside him has yet to speak. I pay attention to him and how he looks at Tom. It hits me like a light bulb going off. He belongs to Tom. He's completely enamored with him. Ryker doesn't know his best friend is dating another man.

"How long have you two been dating?" I ask quietly as Tom and Ryker make conversation with each other.

The male looks at me and smiles sincerely. "Three years. I'm Raul, by the way." He offers his hand, and we shake.

I watch as Tom wraps his arm around Raul, forgetting who he's sitting with. Ryker's eyes widen comically. "Why didn't you tell me?"

"He hasn't told anyone," Raul answers for him. "Three years and I've been his little secret. My Christmas wish this year was to finally be out in the open."

"And I'm tired of hiding the man I love. You did me a favor when you hijacked that stupid dating app." Tom laughs.

"Your mom is going to have a stroke."

"Fuck her if she can't accept me for who I am and who I love," Tom says vehemently.

"Good for you," I tell him. Then I look at Ryker. "I guess there are a lot of Christmas wishes being granted this year."

Ryker has asked me every day what I'd wish for. Then, he goes above and beyond to make them happen. No man has ever treated me like he does. Like I'm precious.

His job as a bouncer is fine with me. He could be jobless, and I wouldn't care. His tattoos are so damn sexy. One of my wishes, which I hope comes true, is my mother's acceptance. She'll support my choice if she wants me to be as happy as she claims.

What will I do if she doesn't like Ryker? I've been so wrapped up in him that I haven't given it much thought. Now, when he's about to meet her, I can't help but question myself.

"Did you want to follow us to the house?" Tom asks, pulling me from my reverie.

Ryker looks at me. "I've never been there. So that's fine with me."

"Isn't this your grandmother's party?" Tom questions me.

"Step grandmother." I corrected him. "I've only met the woman twice in as many years."

"Well then. Shall we go?" Ryker slides out of his chair and helps me stand. We leave the coffee house and wait for Tom and Raul to pull their car around.

The drive is a decent one. Ryker and I are mostly silent, but it's comfortable. Upbeat Christmas music fills the silence, and I smile as I take in the scenery around me.

Christmas has always been my favorite holiday. Mom could never afford expensive gifts, but I didn't care. I just love the sights and sounds.

I used to love seeing the twinkling lights decorating houses. I'd imagine when I was older. I'd have a grand spruce tree gracing my living room, decorated with multi-colored baubles.

I wanted a mantle decorated with garland and stockings. A fire would roar in the hearth, and the house would smell like freshly baked gingerbread.

"What are you thinking about so hard over there?" Ryker's voice cuts into my thoughts.

"Christmas," I respond. "All the wishes I had when I was a child."

Ryker takes my hand and interfaces our fingers. He lifts both to his lips and kisses my knuckles. "Tell me about your wishes."

I do. I get caught up in telling every detail I ever imagined. Ryker smiles and laughs at my girlish dreams. It feels so good to have someone care about my wants, even if they were born from a child's mind.

The conversation makes the trip pass quickly; we're approaching a palatial estate before I know it. The driveway is lined with beautiful greenery wrapped in white lights. There are too many cars to count, and a valet stands ready to take the keys.

Ryker walks around and opens my door for me. Once we're standing on the walkway, he pauses. "Fuck." He mumbles.

"Is everything okay?" I ask just as Raul and Tom join us.

"Yeah. Yeah, everything is fine." He assures me. I know he's lying. He may not be comfortable in this type of environment. I'm not.

"Let's get this over with," Ryker calls out, sounding resigned. He looks like he's walking to his death.

Ryker

My heart drops when I see the house come into view. Fate must be an evil bitch to let me meet the woman of my dreams just to have her be related to the people behind those walls.

"Everything okay?" Sydney asks me.

"Yeah. Yeah, everything is fine." I lie. Nothing is fine. Nothing will ever be okay again once I step foot through the door.

"Let's get this over with," I tell my girl and my best friend.

Tom comes forward, matching my steps, while Sydney stays with Raul. "It's going to be okay." He tells me.

"A little warning would have been nice," I tell him angrily.

"When would have been a good time for that? When you hacked my computer or disappeared into your love bubble?" He asks.

"You were going to have to face them eventually." He reminds me.

"Not today. Not when I haven't had a chance to tell Sydney about my past." I whisper yell.

"And who's fault is that?"

"I know I'm a fuckup. I always have been. Always will be." I criticize myself.

"Fuck that, man. Don't do this to yourself. Stacey wouldn't let you hold on to this blame. Walk in there with your head held high. What happened ... Was. Not. Your. Fault."

Tom's been telling me the same thing for years now. He'd say to stop holding the blame even from behind bars. I can't let it go, though. My little sister may still be alive if not for me.

Suppose I had just taken her and left instead of letting my temper get the best of me. Suppose I'd have taken pictures of the bruises and gone to the state police. There are so many what-ifs.

The only thing that matters is that I didn't do any of those. Instead, I went in guns blazing. I knew my sister was traumatized, and once her husband was beaten and crippled, she wouldn't leave him willingly.

I could have hidden her away from him: her and my niece. Families wouldn't have been completely broken and devastated.

I deserved what I got. Hell, jail time wasn't enough punishment. Is Sydney my current punishment for my past?

Sydney meets us on the porch and laces her arm with mine. She rings the doorbell. A distinguished-looking butler opens the door. It all seems so ostentatious now that I've spent so long on the other side of this much wealth.

"Miss Rothchild." The butler greets with a slight tilt of the head.

"It's Collins. My name is Collins."

The butler ignores her. He greets Tom as well and then ushers us in the house. People mill about in their finest day-drinking attire.

A string quartet plays Christmas carols in the corner. Servers pass around finger food and champagne trays like it's not early afternoon. It's five o'clock somewhere, I tell myself when I grab two drinks from a passing tray. I down both in quick succession before grabbing another.

Sydney touches my face and forces me to look at her. "What's going on?"

"It's nothing," I reply.

"Bullshit. Talk to me, Ryker." She whispers.

I grab her hand and move to pull her down the hall. I need to find somewhere quiet if I'm going to spill all the drama to her.

We don't make it ten feet before a voice calls, "You aren't welcome here."

I turn and face my father. Standing with him is the woman that I once called mom. She looks at me with fear. Of course, she would. I'm not the same person I was six years ago.

"I invited him." Sydney defends. She doesn't know who she's talking to, and my dad won't care who she is. She's a woman and should just keep her mouth shut.

"Syd, don't," I warn. To my parents, I say, "Merry Christmas to you too, Dad. Mom."

Sydney gasps beside me. I try to ignore her, unwilling to lose eye contact with my father. I won't show him weakness or give him the authority he seeks.

"Who is this woman?" My mother asks.

"His girlfriend," Tom responds to her. "Sydney Collins, meet Mr. and Mrs. Ryker Carmichael, Sr." He then says, gesturing between them.

"It's nice to meet you." Sydney politely says.

"Oh, Syd, you're here. And look, you've met Tom." A woman who looks like an older version of my angel says brightly, completely misreading the room.

Everyone falls silent when Warren Rothchild steps into view. "Carolyn, dear." He says as he wraps his arm around Sydney's mother.

He eyes me, then looks down at my hand entwined with his stepdaughter's. His eyes light up. "Ryker, I had heard you'd been released. Shame they didn't keep you longer. Behind bars is where you belong."

"What's he talking about?" Sydney whispers, suspicion in her voice.

"I can explain." I plead.

"Oh. Didn't you know Sydney? You're dating a murderer. Isn't that right, Ryker? You're the reason my son is dead." Warren, Sydney's stepfather accuses.

I look at Sydney. I see the horror shining in her eyes. "And don't forget about your poor sister. She's dead because of you as well." Warren tacks on, digging the knife that much deeper into my heart.

"Is that true?" Sydney inquires. "Tell me it's not true, Ryker."

Instead of responding, I remember the last month I spent with her. I think about all the good that we've shared. And then I see our future go up in flames.

Sydney pulls away from me. She backs up several steps, bumping into Tom. He grips her to steady her. Her mother walks up to her and has a quiet but intense conversation with her daughter.

Once that conversation is done, Sydney turns and runs away right out the front door. I ran to follow her, not wanting her to leave. I need to explain. When I get outside, she's nowhere to be seen. I walk around the massive property, trying to find her unsuccessfully.

Sighing, I give up. I saw the look on Syd's beautiful face. It was a look of regret. She regrets meeting me. As much as I want to go to her house and shake her until she listens, I feel it's better to stay away.

Today proves I don't deserve any happiness. It was childish to believe in Christmas wishes. A man like me doesn't have his wishes come true.

Ryker

January

It's been one month since the disaster of a party at the Carmichael estate. I sit in my living room, beer in hand, staring ahead at the presents sitting under the tree I've yet to take down. The pine needles have started falling off causing a lot of the branches to look bare. Every present under the tree is for Sydney.

She'd tell me all about her wishes for Christmas or special memories she shared with her father and I'd go out the next day and buy her something to represent them. An author journal. A mink throw in rainbows. A Prada bag because the one she got when she got her first royalty check now sits in the bottom of her closet frayed and unusable. A platinum necklace with a small snowflake because she's always loved them.

"You should get rid of those," Tom says when he walks through my door with dinner.

"No."

"Come on man. She won't take your calls. Won't answer her door. It's over."

I refuse to believe that. I know I should have told her about my past. But I was so caught up in the bubble, it didn't cross my mind. That was my mistake.

Hers was not waiting to talk about things. Instead of giving me a chance to explain, she ran. She believed what they told her and then she blocked me. Now, I've spent the past month getting drunk and wallowing.

"Come on, man. Eat and then we're going out."

"You never told me how things went after I left that party."

Tom laughs. "Do I have to tell you? I mean, you know those people. My mother loved Raul but is in denial about my relationship with him. She thinks we're just friends."

I snort at that. Of course, she does. The pretentious bitch.

"But, on a good note, your wish is finally coming true. I'm moving out." He informs me.

"Good for you," I reply. At least something in one of our lives is going right. "I'm still pissed that you didn't tell me."

"What do you want me to say? I was scared."

"I'm your best friend man. I'd never judge. The heart wants what the heart wants." I shrug.

Which is why I can't return those presents. It's why I can't let go of Sydney. Because my heart wants her. Every part of me wants every part of her.

"Do you work this weekend?" Tom asks.

"Yeah."

"I still don't understand that job."

"I enjoy it."

I came clean to Tom a couple of weeks ago and told him that I was the brains behind the background checks for that stupid dating app. I also let him know that I've been working remotely since I got out of prison. Working as a bouncer is just something I do to pass the time.

And I do enjoy it. I like to protect people and what better way to do that than working at one of the places that are breeding grounds for men that prey on women? I couldn't save my sister, but I can help protect other women.

Tom sighs. "You're a bouncer because you still feel guilty."

"No." I deny. "Okay. Maybe."

"Dude. You live in a penthouse apartment that costs more than my mother's house and you drive a car that costs six figures. Yet, you work at a bar, dress like a thug, and drink like a damn fish."

"Damn. Harsh much?" I ask.

"The truth hurts. Just suck it up and go see her already."

"Sydney doesn't want anything to do with me. She made that pretty clear when she ran out on me and blocked me as soon as she got the chance."

Tom sighs. "You grew up in that crowd. What did you expect her to do? Defend you? Man, she had no clue about your past."

True. She didn't. But to not even give me a chance to explain? She just listened to her asshole stepdad.

Technically I didn't kill anyone. Not like I didn't want to. Instead, I just made sure, that had he not punked out and taken his own life, he would have suffered.

Of course, that's not how things went. Instead, I lost my sister, my parents, and years of my life. Now, I have lost the woman I love.

"Okay. Finish up and shower. We're going to go have dinner." Tom orders.

"Okay. Okay. You realize you nag as much as a wife, right?"

"Yep." He retorts, cheerfully. "Now go home. We'll pick you up in an hour."

"Well?"

"Me and Raul. If I have to babysit you and make sure you eat, then I might as well do it while staring at my gorgeous boyfriend."

I can't help but laugh at him. I'm truly happy for my best friend, even if I'm a miserable bastard. If anyone deserves love, it's Tom.

I go back to my apartment and shower like I was told. Tom didn't say where we were going so I dress in a Hensley shirt and a pair of strategically ripped jeans. I want to place a beanie on my head but think better of It.

Now that I'm ready, I sit here and think more about Sydney. I remember the first night I met her and how beautiful I thought she was. There was just something about her that drew me in.

Then the night at the hotel when I pleasured her and then revealed myself. While most women would have felt scandalized, she seemed relieved that it was someone other than Tom. I thought that said something about how she felt about me.

I was so fucking stupid and I wish that my head and heart could get on the same page. But no, my heart is broken and aching for Sydney. My entire body recoils at the thought of moving on.

I'm so royally fucked. In two months I gave my heart to her. And she crushed it beneath her feet.

The bell rings alerting me that Tom and Raul are here so I grab my jacket and head out. The snow on the ground and the ice on the cement slow my pace, but I reach Tom's car without incident.

"Hey, man." Raul greets me as soon as my ass hits the seat.

"Sup?" I question. "Where are we going anyway? Tom never said."

" A new place over on fifth. They're supposed to have amazing wings." Raul answers.

He's such a guy. I laugh to myself with the thought. This guy seems like the total opposite of Tom. He always talks about hiking and biking, trying to get Tom to agree to join him.

He'd have better luck asking the sun to rise in the west. My best friend is not the outdoorsy type. He used to whine about football. He only played because his mom made him.

I'm thankful for it since he saved my ass on the field several times. He was good. Could have gone pro if he wanted.

But that's not him. He prefers being behind a screen working numbers. Or playing video games.

From what I understand, Raul is some sort of private investigator. He doesn't do the whole finding evidence on a cheating spouse or whatever. He's more the person who works cold cases that the cops have given up on.

Tom says he's stellar at that as well. He's helped solve dozens of cases and in this city that means something. He sympathizes with me because he knows law enforcement here sucks.

The more I get to know the guy, the more I like him. Especially for Tom. "We're here." Raul pulls me from my thoughts.

We get out a block away from the restaurant. Traffic in this part of town is insane. As we walk, I see a familiar head of hair ahead of us.

"You know what? This was a bad idea." I say and turn to go.

Tom grabs my arm, halting me. He looks to where my eyes are now. He offers me a look full of pity. That look makes my heart shrivel in my chest.

"You can't avoid life because of one girl," Tom says, patting me on the shoulder.

He doesn't try to stop me when I ignore him and walk away.

Sydney

Tina has been up my ass to get out of the apartment for weeks. My mom has now joined in. It's gotten a little ridiculous.

I don't want to go out. I'm in constant fear of seeing Ryker, plus I have a looming deadline I have to meet or my publisher is going to drop me.

Tina can be extremely persuasive which is how I find myself walking in a crowded area of town heading to the newest, trendiest restaurant in the city.

I should be proud of myself. I even got dressed today. That sounds funny, but it's true. Since the Christmas party, I've sat around in sweats or pajamas.

I haven't even cleaned the house. Thank goodness for my best friend. She hired someone to come in and clean. Though it was embarrassing for anyone to see the state of my space.

There's a small crowd of people standing on the sidewalk and we work to merge ourselves amongst them. A tingling sensation down my neck makes me think that I'm being watched. I try to surreptitiously look around me, but it's hard to see through all the people.

Suddenly, out of nowhere, I hear his voice. My head snaps back around and I crane my neck to find him. He's with Tom and Raul and it looks like they may be arguing. At the very least, Ryker is heated.

"You can't avoid life." I hear Tom say but I block out everything else when Ryker locks his eyes to mine. It's as if he's looking straight into my soul and can see every part of me.

When he turns and rushes away, my heart drops. Tina grabs me and forcefully turns me around, but that doesn't stop Tom and Raul from coming our way.

"You!" Tom yells. "You need to do something about that." He points behind him.

"He lied to me." I hiss.

"Did he? Because as I recall, you never allowed him to explain."

"Was he in jail?"

"Yeah. He was."

"Then that's all I need to know." I retort.

"You're such a bitch." Tom says, "And I'm so glad I dodged a bullet when Ryker hacked my account."

"Aren't you gay?" Tina asks, because of course she has no filter.

"That wasn't the point," Tim responds. "If you aren't willing to hear him out, you don't deserve him."

We stand there silently for I don't know how long before Tom blurts, "He's in love with you."

"You act like that's supposed to mean something." I am still pissed about everything. I'm more pissed that I didn't listen and ran away like a coward, but my stupid pride won't let me rectify the mistake.

I want him crawling back to me on hands and knees. My mind conjures exactly what he can do from that position.

"I think I've lost my appetite," Tom says. "Come on Raul. We can go somewhere else."

Sydney

February First

I've concluded that I am depressed. Or I've known and I've been in denial. It's been almost two months since Christmas. One month since I watched Ryker walk down that sidewalk outside the restaurant.

My mother has summoned me for dinner at her and Warren's house this evening so I'm in my closet looking for something to wear. I won't get away with my standard outfit of jeans and a sweater.

The next month can't come quickly enough. I can't wait to get out of this damn city for a while.

My phone rings from my bed and I pick it up looking at the screen. It's my cousin.

"Tyne!" I exclaim.

"Hey cuz. Are you still heading out this way next month?"

"You know it. I can't wait to meet Amelia and see you."

Tyne met the love of his life at a masquerade ball of all places. I don't know all the details, but it sounds super romantic and I'm glad his father, the asshole, finally got what was coming to him.

"You okay? You got quiet."

"I'm fine. Just tired." I lie.

"Bullshit. What's going on?" He asks. "Your mom called me concerned about you."

I laugh. "My mother is only worried about her reputation and her new husband," I say.

"Yeah. She said something about a guy."

My heart drops. At this point, I think I may have a condition with the number of times my heart twinges and bounces in my chest. "It's nothing I can't handle."

"Do you need me to fly out there and handle him?"

What a clusterfuck that would be. "I appreciate the offer, but no. It's all good. Look, I need to go. If I'm late for dinner, Mom will kill me."

"Alright, little cousin. See you soon?"

"Yep. Send the jet for me."

"I can if you want me to. Just say the word."

"I'll let you know," I inform him.

I hang up and go back to getting dressed. I choose a long burgundy sweater dress with knee-high boots and tights. I throw my hair up in a messy bun and put on light makeup.

If Mom has a problem with the way I look she'll have to get over it. I can't bring myself to put any more energy into my looks tonight.

I grab my purse, phone, and keys and take off to the elevator. My car is sitting in its spot where it always is. I climb behind the wheel and thank all that is holy for the remote start, which has allowed the car to be very toasty.

The drive to Mom's is longer than I'd like and I know she's going to expect me to spend the night. No, thank you. I already booked a room at a little bed and breakfast halfway between there and home.

I pull into the overly bright driveway. Every damn light in the house is on. I guess when you have as much money as Warren, you don't have to worry about the power bill. How many families could just the money he spends on utilities feed?

The door opens before I reach it and the butler stands there ready to take my coat. I don't speak to him, I just hand over my things and then I go straight to the dining room. My mother stands to greet me.

"Right on time." She says, kissing me on the cheek.

"Barely," Warren mumbles from his seat.

"Excuse me?" I question.

Mom gives me no opportunity to continue. She grabs me. "There's someone I want you to meet. This is Jason."

Mom points at a good-looking guy sitting beside Warren. "He's a junior partner at the firm."

Jason stands and shakes my hand. "It's nice to meet you." He smiles.

When I go to my seat, he pulls out the chair, waits for me to sit, and then pushes it in. He passes me the platter of chicken and I use the tongs to grab a leg. Once I've filled my plate, I tuck into my food, determined to end this evening as quickly as humanly possible.

"So, Sydney. Your mom tells me you're an author. Would I be familiar with anything you've written?"

"Not unless you read filth," Warren says. "What do they call it? Smut, I believe."

"Romance." I correct him. "I am a romance author."

"Like the Hallmark movies?" Jason asks, and I'm pretty sure he's only feigning interest.

"Not so clean," I tell him.

He ponders that for a minute. Then a sly smile spreads across his lips. "You write naughty romance." He whispers conspiratorially.

I whisper back. "Extremely naughty." I wink and we both laugh.

My mother smiles and I sober. Was I just flirting with Jason? I quickly finish my food, only speaking when directly spoken to. My mother's mood plummets as time goes on and Jason must have picked up my mood because he hasn't tried to talk to me again.

Instead, he's talked to Warren about work. I kind of feel bad since Warren talks down to him as if he's a child. The more I sit here, the more I wonder if Tom was speaking the truth. If Ryker was. Maybe there is more to the story where he's concerned.

"I was thinking," My mother says. "There's that Spring Spritzer for the office coming up. Perhaps you two could go together."

I balk at the idea. "Mom." I hiss.

"Oh come on, Sydney, it wouldn't hurt you to get out of that apartment and have some fun."

And with that, I'm done. I get up, thank them for dinner, and walk away. "Aren't you staying the night? It's a long drive back." Mom calls.

"I reserved a room. Goodnight Mom." I call back.

My car is waiting in the driveway when I exit the house. I'm almost there when a hand touches my shoulder. I jerk around.

"I'm sorry," Jason says. "I didn't know when they invited me it was for a setup."

"Don't worry about it. I'm used to it from my mother."

"She told me a little about your last relationship. I know she overstepped, but I think she meant well. If it makes you feel better, I'm not looking for a match.

Tilting my head to the side, I take Jason in, wondering how truthful he's being. He lifts his hands and steps back. "I'm being serious. I went through a nasty divorce about a year ago. I'm concentrating on myself and what I want. I don't have time to date."

"Then why did you come here tonight?"

"For a home-cooked meal. It's been months since I've had one." He says.

"And you don't have a mother to cook for you?" I snap.

"She lives in Nevada with my ex."

"Huh?" I ask confused.

"What can I say?" he shrugs. "My life is a country song. She got the house, the car, the dog, my mom, and the baby."

"You have a kid?" I ask.

"I do. She's three. Would you like to see a picture?" He doesn't wait for my answer. He pulls his wallet out and removes a picture.

In it, there's a cute-as-a-button little girl with brown ringlets of hair and freckles across her nose. "She's beautiful. So why aren't you there with her? Sorry, that was intrusive."

"No. It's okay. I was offered a promotion that I couldn't pass up. Everything I do is for my little girl. I'm working on fighting for custody. This job is going to help make that possible."

As much as I don't want to admit it, that makes sense and he seems extremely sincere. I can be friends with a guy, right?

"So friends?" He asks. "And while I won't push you to, would you go to the Spring Spritzer with me? I'm required to be there and I'm afraid your mother has taken me on as a project. She won't stop if I don't have a date will she?"

I think back to how forceful she was back at Christmas and I shake my head. "No. She isn't one to give up easily. Give me your phone."

He hands it over and I put my number in and then call myself from his phone so that I have his number as well. I hand his phone back. "Now you have my number. Send me the details."

He smiles wide. "Thank you. Thank you. Thank you." He says, hugging me. "I owe you."

"Yes. You do." I say.

Jason opens the car door for me and when I get in, he closes it behind me. I'm fucking exhausted from this one dinner and can't wait to get to the B&B and fall into bed.

Ryker

Valentine's Day

Fuck. I hated this day before but I hate it even more now. Especially because I've been summoned to some Spring Spritzer thing at my dad's firm. He has worked for years with Warren Rothschild. At one point they were best friends. Now, their relationship is strained.

You'd think Warren would be fine with my dad considering he has nothing to do with me unless it's an absolute necessity. I can't fathom why he wants me at this thing. Good news, Tom and Raul will also be in attendance.

We were both slated to take over for our parents one day. His mom and both of my parents are on the board of executives. For the time being, Tom does all the accounting for the firm. It's no small task to keep up with a multi-billion dollar conglomerate. I imagine that had I still been a part of my family, I'd have been running the tech department.

They don't even realize that I still do all their behind-the-scenes tech. As far as they're concerned I'm nameless and faceless. They only see my business name and my portfolio. I find it really funny since they pay me a tremendous amount of money even though they cut me from the family fortune.

"I'm surprised you agreed to go to this thing. You know it likely won't end well." Tom says as we drive together.

"I am a sucker for punishment." I joke. "Honestly, I wouldn't go, but Mom asked."

"And you've never been able to deny her." He replies.

"No. I haven't. I think she's trying to bridge the divide."

"Yeah. And what happens when your dad finds out?" He asks.

"He can get fucked." I grunt. "Mom's the only one I give a shit about."

"I get that, man. I just don't like seeing you get beat down." He tells me.

"I know. You're a good friend Tom. Are we picking up Raul?"

"Nah. He'll meet us there."

The office building never changes. It's been the same on the outside as it has been since I was a small child. Walking through the door, I try to make out any differences. I don't see many. I've never understood why they refuse to update it.

The walls are an ugly beige that lacks any imagination. The chairs, while newer, still look old. Everything is dark mahogany. I'm surprised anyone would want to visit this place for business or anything else.

Taking the elevator up to the thirtieth floor, I look at myself in the mirror-like surface of the doors. Dressed in khakis and a polo, I look like

I'm headed to the country club. However, my tattoos stand out on my skin. My dad will hate that I don't have them covered. More's the pity.

The door opens up onto a large open space. Tables are scattered throughout and waitstaff scurry around carrying trays laden with appetizers and drinks. I take it all in with an air of boredom. It doesn't impress me nearly as much as it seems to impress the others who have been invited here today.

Tom taps me on the shoulder and points out my mother in the crowd. When she sees me, she rushes to my side. "Son." She says.

"Hey, mom," I reply. "Any idea why I'm here?"

"None. Your father doesn't tell me anything. He just said you were invited. That it was important you were here today."

"On Valentine's Day? Who decided to do this today of all days?"

"Your father and Warren." She whispers. "I don't have a good feeling about this." She tells me and I know that my mother's intuition is always correct.

I should have listened to my gut. The churning I've been dealing with all morning just backs up what my mother is saying. I decide to try and sneak out before my father sees me, but I'm too late.

Not only does he notice me, but so does Warren. So much for hoping to have a confrontational day. "Ryker." My father says using his business tone.

"Trey," I respond. If he can pretend I'm not his son, I can do the same. "I wish I could say it's good to see you, but my mother raised me to never lie. I need a drink." I say walking away.

Tom is right on my heels as I make my way to the bar. I am stopped in my tracks by a laugh that I would know anywhere. Sydney is standing by the bar laughing at something. No someone. Her eyes meet mine and she gasps, "Ryker."

I look at her, then at the man she's with. The man that has his hand on her lower back like they're very well acquainted. Does he know how she tastes? Or how she likes to be handled a little roughly?

"Ah. I see you've met our newest junior partner, Jason. Wasn't that position supposed to be yours?" Warren snickers.

I turn on him and my fist swings out before I can consider the consequences. Warren's head snaps back and when it comes forward again blood is running down his face. He's livid and I almost expect him to retaliate.

Instead, he does something worse. "I see you still have the same violent streak that killed my son. They should have locked you away for good."

"You know that's not what happened." Tom defends.

"Did he not beat my son until he became crippled? That's why he took his own life. He didn't want to be a burden on his poor mother."

I look over at Sydney and then back at Warren. "Yes, I beat him. But.."

I'm not given a chance to say anything else as the cops come and pull me away. "You're under arrest." One says.

The words go through one ear and out the other as I watch Sydney- tears in her eyes- allow another man to comfort her. She still doesn't believe that Warren isn't telling the full truth.

The last thing I see is Tom talking with Sydney and Jason. I close my eyes and go limp in the officer's hands. Let them lock me away. It doesn't even matter anymore.

Sydney

March

Two days and I'll be on a jet headed for fun and relaxation in Gatlinburg. I havent' been there since I was a child and I'm so excited to see what's changed. Tyne has been sending me messages all week about places that we need to go and things we need to try. There's something called trashcan nachos that sounds so good.

Tyne and I were always close. Even as he went off to take over the family distillery, we kept in touch. I'm proud of him and the man he's become. I can't wait to meet the lucky woman who stole his heart. Amelia sounds lovely and

I've been teasing them that I'm going to write their story one day.

I'm packing my bags, ensuring I have everything I'll need. I finished my latest manuscript yesterday and sent it to my editor. Normally, she'd call me when it's ready and I'd go pick up the printed pages that always bleed with red ink. This time, I've told her that she'll either have to send them to me through email or wait until I get back. Of course, she didn't want to deal with the publisher so she agreed.

I have a few weeks with no obligations to anything or anyone but myself and I can't wait. I'm burnt out. My mental health is starting to decline and this vacation will help. The doorbell ringing catches my attention and I go answer it.

"Delivery for Sydney." The young man says handing me several boxes.

I take them and set them on the table while he helps with the ones that won't fit in my hand. "Hold on just a sec and I'll get you a tip," I tell the delivery guy.

"It's been handled." He says with a huge smile. Alrighty then.

He wishes me a good day and leaves. I walk over to the table and look over the packages. There's no return address, and the boxes are discreet enough that I don't know what they are. My first thought is my mom, so I call her. "Did you order stuff and have it shipped here?'

"Of course not, dear. How's Jason?"

"Can we have just one conversation where you don't ask about my personal life or lack thereof?"

"Dear, I just worry about you. You aren't getting any younger and I'd like to have some grandbabies."

I laugh and then laugh some more. "I don't want children, mother." I'd probably just fuck them up.

"You can't be serious, Sydney." She says and I know an argument is coming.

"Mom. I gotta go. My publisher is calling." I hang up before she can say something else.

I throw my phone on the sofa and watch it sink into the cushions. Good. That's an excuse not to answer when she surely calls back. I re-think that, knowing I need the fucking device that holds all of my important information.

I dig it back out and send a message to Tina. Then another gets sent to Tyne, and they deny knowing anything about the packages as well. If they didn't send them, then who did?

I lift the first box and open the lid. Moving the tissue paper out of the way, I find a note. I lift it out of the box and notice the book sitting in the bottom. I gingerly pull it free and turn it over in my hands. I know without opening the cover it's a first edition copy of Alice in Wonderland.

I begged my parents for a copy every year at Christmas from the time I turned twelve until I was sixteen. Every year I was disappointed. Tears converge in my eyes. I know exactly who sent this. I set the book and the note I've yet to read to the side and pull out another box.

Each one of them contains my Christmas wishes. Things as stupid as a Hello Kitty plush blanket to tickets to my favorite Broadway show. There's one box left and I don't have the heart to open any more of them on my own. I place it and the letter in my carry-on telling myself I'll look at them once I'm with someone I trust because that small little box is going to break me. I just know it.

Wiping the tears from my eyes, I call Tyne. "Send the jet," I say.

"Is everything alright?" He asks me worriedly.

"I don't know," I tell him honestly.

"Be at the airstrip in two hours." He tells me.

We hang up and I grab my things. I snap pictures of all the gifts. There are twenty in total. Twenty-one if you count the one that hasn't been opened yet. I leave them all on the table and head out.

One week later

"Ready to talk about it yet?" Tyne asks as we sit on the sofa watching some documentary.

"Not really. I promise when I am, you'll be the first to know." I try to smile but fail.

"Get up. We have dinner plans." He says. "Amelia is looking forward to meeting you and I can't keep making excuses."

"I never asked you to." I point out. "And you haven't had to spend time stuck here with me."

"I know that. But you're family. The only one outside of Mom I care about, so of course I'm going to be here."

I sigh, but sit up. "Fine. Let's go out. Maybe the mountain air will help clear my head."

"That's a girl," Tyne says, pulling me into a hug. "I love you little cousin."

"I love you too."

Amelia is everything Tyne said she is and more. She's so sweet, but she's also quite the ballbuster. I've decided she's my spirit animal and I want to be her when I grow up. Her friend Carrie is amazing as well.

When Tyne said we were going out, I didn't realize it would be with a crowd. That's not fair. It's just Tyne, Amelia, Carrie, Chad, and me. They're all so in love that I feel out of place being alone.

Amelia notices my discomfort and squeezes my hand. "If you don't want to stay, I can call you an Uber."

"I don't want to offend anyone," I tell her.

She giggles, "Believe me, we won't take offense. I don't know what's bothering you, but I can almost bet it has to do with a man. Am I right?"

I nod, "Yeah. It's complicated."

"It always is. Look, I know we just met and all, but if you need someone to talk to, I have a good ear and an even better shoulder."

"I appreciate that," I say.

"Come on." She orders sliding out of her seat." Let's get you that Uber."

She kisses Tyne and tells him I'm going to head home. She waits with me until the Uber arrives and doesn't head back into the restaurant until we've pulled away from the curb. I know now what she went through with her ex and I consider talking to her.

All I want are my pajamas and bed. I walk through the quiet house heading to the back where the guest room sits. I love what Tyne has done with the place. It was once our grandfather's. Tyne inherited it when he passed away.

He lightened the wooden walls and updated everything. It used to be dark and almost dingy, but now it's light and airy even at night. I grab a bottle of water out of the little miniature refrigerator in my room and sit on the bed. The bag where the box and note are torments me, and I know I won't sleep until I see what it says.

I grab it from the bag along with the box and sit it on the bed in front of me. My hands shake when I reach for the paper. I hold it and take a deep breath. Then, I unfold it and start reading the words.

Sydney,

I'm not sure why I'm even bothering with this letter, but here I am, putting my thoughts and feelings on paper. The gifts have been sitting under a Christmas tree I haven't been able to get rid of until now. They're yours to do with as you see fit. Keep them, donate them, give them away. Burn them for all I care.

Seeing you again was both wonderful and horrible. It was wonderful because, for just a moment, I got to stand in your presence and breathe you in one more time. Horrible, because you were with him, Jason.

The way he touched you, and the way you were laughing with him were more than enough proof that you no longer care for me. That's okay. I just want you to be happy.

I still dream of you. I'll never forget Halloween or the night in the hotel. Do you remember? The way I touched you, tasted you. I hope Jason can be whatever you need.

I know you've opened all the gifts but the smallest box. That one scares you. Don't be afraid sweetheart. Open it now.

I do as the letter says and open the box. Inside is a necklace. I pluck it out and notice that it's half a heart. I look back to the note.

This is what I wanted to offer to you. I planned to give it to you on Christmas morning while I explained that what was left of my heart is yours. You see, I can't give you all of it because my sister took the other half with her when she died.

I do not claim to be a good man or even one deserving of you, but there is a reason behind my actions years ago. Warren told you that I was responsible for his son's death and I'll admit that in a way I was. What he failed to mention is that his son killed my sister.

You see, my parents were always close to the Rothschilds and we grew up together. My sister

Stacey fell in love with their son which was kind of perfect for our families. Things were good for a time and they got married. That's when things changed.

I was in the Army, away a lot. Stacey would write me letters and tell me all about her life including the parts that she wanted to keep hidden from the public. When I finally came home for good, I saw the marks.

Travis took things too far and beat her so badly that she ended up in the hospital. She told them she'd fallen down the stairs, but I knew. I knew he was hurting her and I couldn't let it continue.

He needed to learn a lesson, and everyone refused to do anything. There were calls recorded to the police. So many domestic calls that they never even investigated because of who Travis was, and who his father is.

I went to their house and he and I fought. I was beating his ass when he fell and hit the table. It severed something and crippled him. I didn't mean for that to happen, but I knew something no one else did.

Stacey was pregnant with my niece. I was convicted of using excessive force and sentenced to jail time. My family stopped talking to me. Even my sister ignored me. Now she was all alone with this man who could never walk again, and I wasn't there to protect her.

One night while she was bathing, he wheeled himself into their room and removed a revolver from the bedside table. Stacey had been listening to music so she didn't hear him and she never saw the gun. He put a bullet in the back of her head and then turned the gun on himself.

A neighbor heard the shots and called the police. By the time they got to the house, it was too late to even save the baby.

So yes, I am responsible. I was a caring brother in a shit situation and I made it worse. It's my fault that my sister is dead and I carry that guilt with me daily. I feel it every hour of every day.

I understand why you ran away. I don't blame you because heaven knows I don't deserve to be loved. I don't even love myself.

But I do love you. I fell so fucking hard for you. I need you to know that. I need you to know that I will probably always love you even if you never reciprocate those feelings.

Can I tell you my wish? It's a simple one. My wish is that you are always happy and feel the love you are so deserving of. I hope that you can offer that same love to someone in return one day. So I'm letting you go.

At another time, in another place, we could have been great. Hell, we were great *for a short while. Don't let your mom or anyone else dictate your life okay? Promise me. Be undeniably you, always. Because everything you are is beautiful.*

Yours,
Ryker

Sydney

"What are you doing lying here in the dark? Did something happen?" Tyne asks when he enters the house. Amelia is behind him and when she sees the note I still hold in my hand, she comes over.

"Tyne, give us a few minutes, will you?" She asks.

"Sure. I'll meet you upstairs." He tells her. "Goodnight cousin." He says to me.

Once we're alone Amelia takes the note. I don't try to stop her as she reads the words Ryker bled across the paper. "Oh, sweetheart." She says sympathetically, pulling me into her side.

I thought the tears were finally drying up, but when she wraps her arms around me they begin to stream down my face again. "It's going to be okay." She says.

"No, it's not. I'm such an idiot." I whine. "How could I have been so dense?"

"Stop that." She chastizes. "Look at me. You didn't do anything wrong. Did Tyne tell you how he and I met?"

I nod. "He told me a little bit."

"Then you know that before him, I was engaged to another man, one that berated me and cheated with my sister."

"Yeah, and?"

"Did he tell you about the woman that tried to come between us and that I ran away?"

I laugh. "No. He left that out."

"I did, though. I ran straight out of the country and he came after me."

"Ryker didn't come after me, Amelia. He let me go."

"Probably because he doesn't know how to fight for what he wants. Sounds to me like nobody ever fought for him. He seems to really love you though, if it's any consolation."

"Wouldn't he have come to talk to me if that were the case?"

"He's a man." She snorts. "Sounds to me like he'd rather see you happy without him. It takes a strong person to let the person they love go."

"Would you let Tyne go if you were in the same situation?"

"Not likely. I'm a weak bitch." Amelia says jokingly. "In all seriousness, if I thought he'd be better off without me, then yes, I love him enough that I'd let him go."

"Good thing I'd never let you go then," Tyne says from the doorway. "I just wanted to make sure you two were okay."

"We're good. I was on my way up." Amelia tells him, kissing him.

Tyne looks me over and grimaces. "I hate to see you hurting. Do I need to kick his ass?"

That gets me laughing. "I think you'd meet your match in this one. Likely get your ass handed to you."

Hugging me, Tyne whispers. "You're how many miles away from him? You should text him or call him."

"No." He doesn't want to hear from me."

"I'll take that bet. He doesn't know where you are, right?"

I shake my head. "Not even Mom knows I'm visiting you."

"Good. Then he can't get to you here if you don't want to see him. Just call him, Syd. I have a feeling you'll regret it if you don't."

"I'll think about it," I answer.

Tyne hugs me again and bids me a goodnight. Then he's gone. Off to be with his woman.

Ryker

I know Sydney got the gifts. I paid the delivery guy a premium to report back to me once they were in her hands. It didn't feel right to keep them and it felt even worse to consider taking them back. The only other option was to ensure they got to the person they were intended for.

Did she like them? Hate them? Did she throw them all in the garbage?

She got the gifts and then skipped town. I have no way to know where she is or how she's feeling. Did she read the letter? I never expected it to change anything. I know now that she doesn't want to be with me and that's okay. I think.

It hurts a lot more than I'm willing to admit, but it is what it is. I just hope that guy Jason treats her right.

That's a lie. I want to rip his fucking head off. It sucks that he got the girl. He got the job that was meant for me, in a company that is supposed to be my legacy. Not that I care about that. But why does he get my life? What did I ever do wrong to cause karma to fuck me over so royally?

Oh, that's right. I was responsible for my sister and niece's deaths. Well, karma can eat a bag of dicks because it for sure sucks. Just like everything in my life.

Perhaps it's not karma. The anniversary of my sister's death is tomorrow and I feel like everything that's happened the last few months is Stacey's way of getting payback. It makes sense. I took something from her so she takes something from me.

The beer in my hand is getting warm, but I can't let it go because the gun on the table in front of me is much too tempting. Would anyone miss me? I don't think so. Dad would probably rejoice that his good-for-nothing son can no longer smear his good name.

Mom would cry, probably out of obligation so that people don't realize she's being controlled by her overbearing husband. Everyone knows that Warren would likely dance on my grave in celebration. Tom may be the only one who would truly mourn me, but he has Raul to comfort him.

Everyone has someone except for me. I'm all alone. The bottle drops onto the carpet and my hand reaches out, stroking the grip and feeling the cold metal of the barrel. I lift it and put my finger on the trigger. It would be so easy. Just a little squeeze and all this pain inside my chest would be over.

I'd see my sister again. I'd finally get a chance to apologize and beg for her forgiveness. I have the gun pointed at my head when my phone lights up the darkness around me. The name on the screen makes me pause.

It's her. It's Sydney. I put the safety back on the gun and lay it on the table. My whole body shakes with adrenaline as I pick the phone up and look at the message.

I read the letter.

Three little words. But the little periods are going across the screen as if she's typing so I sit back and wait for her next message.

"What the fuck, Ryker!" Tom's voice screams.

I wake up with my head spinning and difficulty remembering last night. When I sit up, my stomach rumbles and I can taste bile in the back of my throat. It's not until Tom grabs my hand that I realize I'm holding the gun and my phone lies in pieces by my feet along with empty beer and liquor bottles.

All at once, the memories of last night come back. The one message that Sydney sent was the only one I received. I waited and when no more came through, I started drinking and didn't stop until there was nothing left.

I recall grabbing the gun and my mind telling me repeatedly that it would all be so much easier and better for everyone if I were gone. I'm not lovable.

My sister stopped loving me because I involved myself in her personal life. Then my parents stopped loving me after her death. Sydney couldn't love me because of my past and the fact I kept it from her.

My best friend pitties me and I'm pretty sure that's the only reason he stays.

"Please tell me you weren't going to do something stupid," Tom yells. "Please." He repeats.

"I can't," I tell him honestly. "Sydney messaged."

"What?"

"She read the letter I sent her."

"And?" He asks.

"And nothing. That's all she said. Couple that with Stacey's death anniversary and it all just fucked with my head." I explain.

Tom takes the gun away and places it far away, then he starts cleaning up the mess I left in my drunkenness. He mumbles under his breath as he works. All things I can't understand.

"It's enough, Ryker. You have to let her go." Tom complains.

In my fuzzy mind, I think he's speaking Of Stacey. "She's my sister." I grit.

"Not her, Ry. Sydney. You need to let go of Sydney."

"But, I love her." I whimper. Me, a grown man whimpering like a baby.

"Clearly she doesn't reciprocate those feelings," Tom says. "And stop being a baby. Get up and get dressed."

"Why? What's the point?"

"Just fucking do it, Ryker. Or I'll drag your sorry ass up."

Not wanting to fight with my best friend, I stand. My legs are shaky and my stomach rolls. I don't know if I've ever been this hungover.

I get dressed without bothering to wash the stench of the alcohol from my body. At this point, it's exiting from every pore. Tom throws me a pair of sunglasses which I gratefully accept when the light of the sun hurts my eyes.

I follow and climb into the passenger seat of Tom's car. I try unsuccessfully to keep my eyes open, and I fall asleep to the noise from the radio and the air from the open windows.

Voices wake me from sleep. I'm still in the car and when I look over I notice that Tom is gone. In front of the car stands a sprawling estate with columns and several stairs. Sitting on the porch with a pretty brunette is Tom.

I open the door and step out. Tom notices me and stops talking. I walk toward them and they both stand.

"Hi, Ryker. I'm Brooke. It's nice to meet you." She sticks her hand out to shake mine.

I take it, give it a quick pump, and release her. "Yeah. You too." I look around me again.

The grounds are perfectly manicured and I notice people meandering the gardens. "What is this place?" I ask.

Brooke looks at Tom and I swear they have a silent conversation. "Perhaps we should sit. I could have someone bring us coffee or tea." She offers.

"Do you have a beer?"

"No. We don't allow alcohol or drugs here."

"Where is here, Brooke?"

"Hope House." She replies.

"This is an intervention, Ryker," Tom explains.

"An intervention for what? Having a few drinks?"

"No. You need help, Ry. I walked into your house and found you lying on the sofa with a damn gun in your hand and broken glass and empty bottles on the floor. I thought at first you were dead."

"God, Tom. I wasn't trying to kill myself."

"Are you sure about that? Because I'm not so certain."

"It was one moment of weakness, man. You know me."

"I thought I did. But be honest with me. Be honest with yourself. You've not dealt with your sister's death or the things that happened after."

"I'm handling it."

"No, you're not. Look, man. You're my brother, even if we don't share blood. If you can look me in the eyes and tell me that you didn't have thoughts of ending it all last night, I'll drop it."

He knows I can't honestly tell him that. I was considering pulling that trigger but I passed out before getting the chance. "I can't," I tell him.

"And that's okay. The first step to healing is being honest about what you're feeling." Brooke says. "That's what we're here for. To help you finally face those feelings safely and healthily."

"She continues speaking for a minute and then says, "Let's show you to your room."

"I can't stay here. I have things to take care of. Besides, I don't have any of my things."

"I packed you a bag and I can't bring you anything else you need," Tom tells me.

"Actually, you can't. This is a closed facility. We don't allow visitors except on designated occasions. I find it best for our residents to go through this process alone. At least for a while."

"That's shitty," Tom tells her.

"Maybe. But it allows our residents to concentrate on themselves and their own needs. That's how they heal."

"Do you truly think this is going to help me?" I ask.

"I hope so. But that will depend on you."

"I don't want to stay here," I whine.

"You can stay willingly and work through your issues, or I'll have you committed through the court. I swear on my relationship with Raul that I will do it, Ryker. You aren't the only one that lost Stacey. I lost her too."

"You think I don't know that?" I ask.

"I know you do. She is your sister. But, Ryker, you are my best friend. You and Stacey are the closest thing to siblings I have and I can't lose you also. I won't."

We go back and forth for a long time. I tell Tom all the reasons this won't work and he tells me all the reasons it will. Eventually, it boils down to a threat. Since he's afraid he'll lose me anyway, he says he'll walk away now and never look back.

Tom is the only one that has ever stood by me. I can do this for him. Even if I have to fake my way through it because there is nothing wrong with me.

"Fine. I'll stay." I give in.

Tom smiles and hugs me. "I promise they will help you." He whispers. I don't believe him, but whatever.

"Good," Brooke says. "Then I'll just show you to your room."

Tom and I say our farewells, he hands me my bag, and we go our separate ways. Him back to his life and me to the unknown.

Sydney

July

The call from Tom kind of came out of nowhere and was surprising for two reasons. The first, Tom and I hadn't spoken in months. Not since Ryker was admitted into Hope House. And second, because he asked me to come with him to Ryker's visitation tomorrow.

I don't know if I can do it. I've missed Ryker something awful and he's never far from my mind. I waited for him to respond to my messages and when I found out why, I felt fucking guilty. Like it was my fault he contemplated suicide. Even after Tom explained everything to me, I still feel like shit.

I should have reached out sooner, I tell myself constantly. That and I shouldn't have run away. Perhaps I fucked up when he saw me with Jason and I didn't explain that we weren't together.

I need to put my big girl panties on and face Ryker, I know. It's just....hard. I thought the trip I took to Gatlinburg would help, but I spent most of the time in tears reading the letter Ryker had sent me over and over.

I read it so much that the ink is smeared and the edges are all crinkled. The letter now sits on my desk as a reminder of words said and others left unspoken. They've been the inspiration for my newest book which seems to flow freely from my fingers to the screen of my computer.

Would Ryker approve of me using his past to inspire me? I somehow feel that by writing all of it down, I can help him put the past to rest. Or is it my own redemption I'm seeking?

"You look tired, dear." My mother says as she hands me a glass of iced tea. "You should be sleeping more."

"I'm fine, Mother."

"You know, it could be all that junk in your pantry making you tired. I keep telling you that stuff isn't good for you. Plus, if you keep eating all of that you won't be able to fit in your dress for the benefit next month."

I ignore her as I've learned over the years to do. She's always going on about my weight or something else that she's not happy with. I don't wear my makeup right. Can't keep a guy interested because I'm not timid enough. A woman should be seen and not heard. Blah, blah, blah.

Even though I ignore it all, that doesn't mean it doesn't hurt. I'll never be a size two, hate makeup unless it's necessary, and there's not a timid bone in my body. All of those things to my mother's utter dismay. Ryker didn't care about any of that.

He would tell me I was beautiful when I was fresh-faced out of the shower. He loved lounging around with me even if I was in frump flannel pajamas all day. And if he had a problem with my size- I'm a size eight- he never once complained when he lifted and pinned me against the wall.

Listening to Mom berate me for the millionth time helps me to decide that I will go with Tom tomorrow. I've met Ryker's parents and I know my stepfather. Tom told me more about Ryker's past and I can see that he went through worse than I ever have. It must have been horrible for him after his sister's death. And to know that his whole family had turned their backs on him makes me sick.

I don't owe him anything, but I do owe it to myself to get closure. Plus, I'd be quite the bitch if I let him go on thinking I hate him. We can be friends, right? Months ago I would have given anything to be with him even after I ran. Now, I don't know.

I mean I still love him, but can I be with someone who has the clear issues he has? You don't just think about suicide one time. It's like a festering disease that causes you to think about it any time things get hard. Ryker accused me of running away, and I did, but he was going to leave everyone.

He gave no thought to who it would affect. Tom would have been devastated and I'm certain that deep down his parents would never want that. Even if they are part of the problems that drove him to the edge.

"Mother, I have a lot of work to do. We'll talk later this week okay?"

"Are you kicking me out?" Mom asks, outraged that I would even consider the thought.

"Mom. I'm not kicking you out. I'm asking you to leave so I can work. I'm on a deadline and if I don't get the next five chapters to my editor by Friday, I'm in trouble."

"Fine." She huffs. "But Warren and I expect you and Jason for dinner on Sunday."

When the door to my apartment closes, I lay my head across my arms and let out a frustrated scream. Of course, I'm expected. Jason and I have become good friends since we met, but that's all it is. Friends.

He joins me for dinners so that I don't have to constantly be reminded that I betrayed some unspoken pact when I dated Ryker. And he uses me so that all the women vying for his attention stay far away.

My phone rings and I place it on speaker, a smile on my face. "Hey, babe." Jason greets.

"Hey, boo. Whatcha up to today?" I ask.

"Taking a much-needed day off. Wanna come out and play with me?"

I laugh. "No can do. I'm swamped with writing."

"Figures. How's that going by the way? Can I read it yet?"

"It's going well and no you can't read it. You have to wait with the masses."

"Damn. Okay." I can hear the pout in his voice. "What about the other thing? Have you made a decision?"

"I think I'm going to go. If I had anything at all to do with his issues, I need to apologize."

"You know none of it is your fault, right? He has some deep-seated issues that he needs to work through."

"I know. I just can't help feeling guilty in a way."

"For what? Being human? Any woman would run away from a man who was accused of murder. That served jail time because of it." Jason says.

"That's just it though. He didn't serve jail time for murder, Jason. He served time for trying to defend his little sister."

"By using his fists. He could have handled it a different way."

"Maybe," I respond. "But what would you have done if that had been you and she was your sister?"

"I'd have killed the bastard."

"Exactly. And maybe Ryker would have done the same, but he didn't. He tried to help his sister and in the end, she still lost her life."

I don't want to argue with Jason about this. The only reason we've even discussed it is because Warren loves to remind me that I was dating a madman, as he puts it. I'm starting to believe that he is.

"Anyway, I'm going to go see what Ryker has to say and apologize for my part in his issues. Then I'm going to tell him we can be friends, come home, and finish writing this damn book."

"Did you want me to come with you?" He asks.

"I don't think that's a good idea," I reply.

I'm riding with Tom and I feel that Jason's presence will just set Ryker back on whatever progress he's made. Plus, if I'm honest with myself, I don't want Ryker to think that Jason and I are an item. Not when in my heart, I want Ryker back.

I won't act on my feelings. I can't. My mother is married to the man who has helped ruin his life. Warren can't see past his perfect son. I believe with my whole heart that Ryker and Tom have been truthful about everything.

I see it now. Every time I look at Warren or hear some snide comment come from his mouth. Hate breeds hate. I wouldn't be surprised if Warren was an abusive son of a bitch himself.

My mother sure knows how to pick them.

Ryker

"Man, it's good to see you," Tom says as he hugs me tight. "You look good. Better than the last time we saw each other."

"I feel good," I respond. "Better than that, actually."

"Good. Good. Let's sit."

"How's everyone? Raul? My mom?"

Tom chuckles. "They're good. Your mom wanted to be here but she didn't think you'd be receptive to her visit."

I sigh. She'd be right. While I've been working on myself, I've determined that I resent my mother for her part in everything that happened. Not that she physically did anything, but she sat back while my father disowned me and she said nothing.

Looking back, she never defended us kids. She had two perfect little dolls to dress up and play house with, but she never handled the tough stuff. She sat quietly and watched it all as if she were watching a film on television.

"Have you spoken to Syd?" I ask.

"We were waiting for you to ask," Tom says.

"We?" I question and Tom points somewhere over my shoulder.

I turn and see Sydney standing in the doorway hesitating to enter the room fully. I stand

and walk to her. I don't embrace her, just look at her. Then I lean down and kiss her on the cheek.

"You're a sight for sore eyes. Thanks for coming."

"Of course." She says, still very hesitant. She looks at the ground instead of at me, which is strange for the girl who legitimately tells things exactly as they are.

"Come sit?" I ask.

She follows me over and takes a seat beside Tom. I hide the disappointment of not having her beside me, or in my lap. My feelings for her haven't disappeared. They haven't dwindled.

If anything, they've grown. I'm learning so much about myself here and another realization I had is that I didn't tell Sydney about my past because I was afraid I'd lose her. I didn't tell her because I was terrified she'd stay.

I didn't know how to handle the fact that I was falling in love with her. I also think I knew that I was too fucked up to give Syd everything she deserves. I couldn't be fully present in our relationship when I was still living in the past.

I'm working on forgiving myself for my actions that led to my sister's death. I journal daily. Just a few thoughts here and there. And lately, I've been writing letters.

That's part of why I asked Tom to bring Sydney if she'd agree. I wrote her another letter and today, the residents ready to leave this place, have to read them out loud. To say I'm nervous about putting it all out there would be an understatement.

Tom tells me everything and it's no secret that Sydney is seeing that Jason guy. Tom's mother has no problem trying to throw it in his face that it could be him with her. He just laughs and reminds her he's gay. She still doesn't believe him.

I won't bring up Jason because it doesn't matter. I've decided I'm still going to read the letter and let Sydney know how I feel. If she chooses to be with him, that's okay. She deserves every bit of happiness. I'd never fault her for that.

I also know that regardless, I'll be okay too. It may take more time to come to terms with it all, but I will. Because for the first time in a very long time, I'm strong enough.

Strong enough to let the love of my life go if that's what she wants.

"Alright, everyone," Brooke calls. "Our residents have been working their programs very hard the past few months. One part of that is writing. We encourage everyone to write their feelings down to give them physicality."

Brooke continues to talk but I can't pay attention. I'm too busy searching for any changes in Sydney since the last time we were together. Her hair is the only thing I notice. More brown than it was, as if she went back to her natural color.

"Ryker, would you start us off please?" Brooke asks, pulling me away from staring.

I stand and make my way up front. Brooke places her hand on my back and rubs it up and down. What would Tom think if he knew one of my therapists has begged me to fuck her on the desk in her office? I ended up asking for a male to work with.

Dr. Echols has been nothing short of amazing and understanding. He's extremely knowledgeable, especially in the science of grief. I don't know his story, but I have a feeling it's drenched in tragedy.

Sydney

Tom didn't prepare me for this part of the program. I thought I'd come, sit and talk to Ryker for a bit, and then leave. I didn't know that he'd be reading a letter.

One he wrote from all the bottled emotions he'd been holding onto. What if his letter is to me and he says how much he hates me? What will I do with that?

Or what if he says he still loves me and wants to be with me? I've been over that option in my mind a hundred times. We were great together, but our families are toxic.

There's too much baggage to weed through between the two of us. His tragic past and my inability to tell my mother to go to hell even though I fully recognize her controlling behavior and manipulation.

I shut all thoughts from my mind. I need to stop worrying. Whatever those letters say, it'll be okay. I can deal with whatever it is.

"When writing down my emotions was first mentioned as a way to deal with the past, I didn't believe it would help. Now, I stand before you all, a man that is healing. I have a very long way to go, but I finally believe I'll get there." Everyone claps and Ryker pauses.

"We were asked to write letters to the people most important to us, those that have hurt us and those we have hurt. I've decided not to read any letters today. They won't change the mistakes I've made or give solace to those I've hurt. All I will say is that I am sorry for being selfish. I promise to try harder for those I care about. But mostly, I promise to keep putting the pieces of myself back together for me."

Another round of applause thunders through the crowd. Ryker looks over all their heads and finds me. Our eyes meet and in that one look, I can see all the love he still holds for me along with the hope that I'll be waiting when he gets out of this place. My throat begins to close and I can't look away.

I try. Damn do I try, because I can't let him see that I share the same hope and love. Those can't be the things reflected in my eyes.

Ryker is the one to break our staring contest when the woman, Brooke, grabs his arm and pulls him away. My body moves of its own accord to follow. I don't know why, but when I get around the corner where they went what I see breaks my heart even if it shouldn't.

Ryker has his hands on Brooke's sides and her arms are wrapped around his neck, their mouths fused. I'm so stupid. It wasn't love I saw in his eyes, it was just my imagination. Of course, he didn't write a letter to me. Why would he when his feelings have changed?

An unbidden gasp escapes causing Ryker to break the kiss. "Sydney." He says. "It's not what it looks like."

"Really, Ryker. I expected better of you. All that talk about healing. I bet you are." I swipe my hand out. "She must be offering you quite the therapy."

I turn on my heel and for the second time, I run away from the man that holds my heart. I'm in an Uber within minutes and headed straight to the airport. I hope Tyne's up for a surprise.

Ryker

"Fuck!" I yell. I turn to Brooke and it takes every bit of willpower I possess not to wring her fucking neck. "What the fuck was that?" I ask.

"I just wanted you to know how I feel." She tells me. "I love you, Ryker."

I laugh. "And I thought I needed therapy. I made it very clear to you that I wasn't interested. I changed therapists so we weren't alone together."

I go to chase Sydney, but I only make it as far as the gathering of people before Tom stops me. "What the hell? Sydney just ran out of here like her ass was on fire."

"She saw Brooke kiss me," I tell him.

"Why was Brooke kissing you?"

"Because she's psychotic. She has it in her head that she loves me."

"Are you serious?" He asks.

"Deadly. I need you to give this to Syd." I hand him the letter I was supposed to read today along with one of my journals. "Please, Tom. I know I've been a shit friend, but I need your help."

"You need to get out of here."

"I know, but it will take a day or two. I have to make arrangements to continue therapy outside of this place."

"Okay. If it's any consolation, I'm proud of the progress you're making. Please keep it up."

"I promise. There's Dr. Echols. I need to go talk to him." I say.

Tom and I quickly say our goodbyes and he leaves. I find the doctor in his office. "That was quite the speech, Ryker."

"Thanks," I reply. "Can we talk for a minute?" I ask.

"By the look on your face, I'd say it's quite important. Come on in and have a seat."

I do as he says and I lay everything out for him. I tell him everything. When I'm done he's just as livid as I am. "I'll make sure that she never sees another patient and her license is revoked."

"I appreciate that. I have a favor. I know I still have a few weeks left in my program but I was hoping to be released early. I plan to find a therapist outside of Hope House."

"No need. I would love to continue our work together. You've made great strides and I do have an office in the city. Would you be willing to see me there twice a week?"

"Twice a week?" I ask.

"To start. We'll see where you are in a few weeks and adjust your program accordingly. And you'll still journal."

"Sure. I can do that."

"Then, Ryker, go pack your bags. There will be a car here for you within the hour."

Once I'm dismissed, he picks up the phone and tells whoever is on the other end that he wants to see Brooke immediately. I would never want to ruin someone's career, but she crossed a line. I could have handled it, but she hurt Sydney, and that I can't abide.

Rushing through my room, I get my things packed and meet the car as it pulls into the driveway. I don't breathe freely again until I see the lights of my apartment building.

Days go by before I hear from Tom again. He's coming over now to talk. There's been no word from Sydney. No word from anyone.

Tom took care of the club and let them know I needed a leave of absence. Carl, my boss, called and wants to know when I'll be back to work. I tell him soon and hang up. I don't know if I will go back.

It's not like I need the money. My business brings in money without me lifting a finger at this point. All I have to do is log in occasionally and screen the new jobs I'm being considered for.

That gives me a lot of time to think and even more time to journal. I've filled three of them since I left Hope House. My appointments with Echols have gone well, and I feel like I'm still making progress.

I can finally go to sleep at night without seeing my sister's battered face. For every harsh thing my father has ever said to me, Echols has offered me affirmations to combat them. I'm even ready to sit down with my mother. If she's willing.

It will likely be a long time before I'm ready to face my old man. But my mother, I can handle. The doorbell dings and I get up to answer it. Tom and Raul stand there together. "Come on in," I say and walk barefoot across the marble to the kitchen. "Can I get you something to drink? Water? Juice?"

"No beer?" Tom asks.

"No beer," I confirm. "No hard alcohol either. Just water, juice, sports drinks, that kind of thing."

"Good," Tom says. "I'm proud of you."

"Thanks."

"I'll take a water if you don't mind," Raul says and I go to the refrigerator. Pulling out a bottle, I hand it to him.

Raul begins to make small talk and I know we're stalling. All of us. "So..." I start.

"She left."

"I know that. I was there." I say.

"No. I mean she left the state again. I don't know where she went, so I couldn't give her the letter or the journal."

I sit forward and place my arms across my knees. It figures. Of course, she left. Probably to the same place she went before.

"Did she leave alone?"

"Are you asking if Jason went with her?" Raul asks. "Because the answer is no. She left alone."

"How do you know?"

"I'm a private investigator and Tom was worried for her so I tracked her all the way to the airport."

"And you don't know where she went?" I ask.

"No. I don't have the authority to get that information and I'm not stupid enough to fuck with the TSA."

"I gotta go," I tell them both. "I need to talk to Jason."

"At eight o'clock at night? Dude, the office is closed. Calm down. You can go see him tomorrow." Tom says. "Let's eat, talk, and not worry about things we have no control over."

He makes a valid point. I let them choose dinner. Raul chooses Cuban because Tom and I have never tried it and he wants us to immerse ourselves in his heritage for a night. I don't argue because I don't care what we eat. I'm not that hungry anyway.

Raul sips on a beer while Tom and I both drink peach mango juice. The guys decide to stay the night, taking advantage of the spare bedroom. We watch a movie and talk for hours before we finally crawl into bed. I'm exhausted. Who knew trying to be a better version of yourself could be so tiring?

Sydney

"It's been two weeks and while I'm always happy to see you, I need to know what brought you here with only the clothes you were wearing," Tyne says, as we drive down the main strip of Gatlinburg. We're heading to a restaurant that offers fondue. It's one of Amelia's favorite places and who doesn't love dipping things in cheese?

"Am I not allowed to surprise my favorite cousin?" I ask.

"I'm your only cousin on your dad's side and yes, you can always surprise me. However, when you show up looking like you were run over and with no bag, no clothes, and no computer you can expect I'll have questions."

"Okay then. What if I say that I don't want to talk about it?"

"Not good enough." He snaps. "Look. You know I love you. And I'm worried about you. You haven't been yourself in months. I thought you were headed back in the right direction when you went home the last time. What is so dire that it could cause this drastic change in you?"

"Fine. So, Ryker admitted himself to a mental health facility." I say.

"Ryker is the bouncer that killed his sister's husband?"

"No. He didn't kill his sister's husband. He put him in a wheelchair. He beat the hell out of him because he was beating the hell out of his sister, Stacey. His sister stopped talking to him. His parents did the same. Then the brother-in-law killed the sister and himself." I expalin.

"That's fucked up."

"Ya think? Anyway, he goes to this facility to get some help because he was contemplating suicide. His best friend found him passed out on the sofa with the gun in his hand."

"Suicide isn't the answer," Tyne says.

"He knows that. That's why he agreed to therapy. He had a visitation the day I came here."

"You went didn't you?"

"I had to."

"You love him." Tyne accuses.

"I thought that was pretty evident."

"So what happened? If you love him shouldn't you be with him right now?"

"I saw him kissing one of the therapists. When he realized I saw it, he said it wasn't what it looked like. When is it ever not what it looks like?"

"When it's not. You know most of my history with Amelia. Have I told you about Felicity and her lies?"

"Yeah. That's what caused Amelia to leave your sorry ass." I snap.

"None of it was true though. Amelia didn't give me a chance to explain before she left me. Sound familiar?"

I huff, then sigh. "Yeah. I guess it does."

"So what are you going to do about it?"

"Nothing. It doesn't matter. Our families are toxic to our relationship, Tyne. Warren has my mom fully believing the lie that Ryker killed his son or was responsible for it. Ryker's parents are either horrible people or are afraid of Warren since he's a big wig in the company they share."

"So cut them out of your lives."

"It's not that simple. I can't just cut my mother out of my life." I argue.

"Of course you can. Your mother is a bitch. She's constantly berating you over the most stupid shit as if you not being model thin or having bottle blonde hair makes you less of a person."

I want to argue that he doesn't know anything but I can't. Because he's right. But my mom is too.

"It doesn't by the way."

"What?"

"It doesn't make you any less of a person. Does Ryker say anything negative about your weight?"

"No. He loves that I have meat on my bones."

"Does he care that your hair isn't dyed?"

"Not that I know of."

"Has he ever criticized the way you dress or how you wear your makeup?"

"Never. He prefers me to be comfortable."

"There you have it," Tyne says. "That man loves you more than your mother ever has. He accepts you for who you are as a woman and not for how you look. He sounds like a really good guy."

The best, I think to myself. "I'm not ready to go back," I tell Tyne.

"Didn't say you had to. You can stay as long as you like. Hell, stay forever. You know I'd love to have you close. Just don't forget that you will eventually have to face Ryker and your other problems. You can't run from them forever."

"I can try," I say.

"You're a brat. Let's go enjoy dinner and then when we get home, I want you to grab my laptop and work on that book."

"Yes, Dad." I snark making Tyne laugh. "I really do need my laptop and the pages I've already worked on. I'll call Jason. Are you cool if he comes and stays for a couple of days?"

"Nope. So long as he isn't trying to hook up with you. I'm kind of rooting for Tyne."

"Why?" I question.

"I think he and I might be kindred spirits."

"Maybe," I say noncommittally. If that's the case, I guess I could do worse.

"You guys are fucking insane." I laugh. After dinner, we all congregated back at the house to play "Cards Against Humanity". I've never played before so I didn't know what to expect, but some of these answers are just hilarious.

"You're one to talk. I've never met a person as morbid as you. I swear you should write horror instead of romance." Carrie says. "Seriously, how's the new book coming"

"Slow," I say. "But that's because I don't have my computer so I've been writing everything the old-fashioned way."

It's the truth. The words are still flowing. At this rate, my publisher will think it's two books instead of one. I still feel a little bad about using Ryker's life as my inspiration, but when I've tried to write anything else, I just feel blocked.

I plan to tell Ryker at some point about the book. I won't let him be bombarded by it when it finally releases. Even if I have to send him a letter or talk to Tom and have him do it for me.

"Tyne tells me you're thinking about moving," Amelia says, starting a completely different conversation that has the table buzzing.

I cut my eyes at Tyne. I never said I was moving here. "I'm not sure where he got that idea. Just because I'm not ready to go home yet, doesn't mean I'm not going to."

"I know, cuz. It's just wishful thinking. I meant what I said. You stay as long as you like." Tyne tells me.

I grab his hand and squeeze it. "I appreciate it, Tyne. I really do."

The game continues for several hours and I finally have to bow out because I'm so tired. I'm not used to being up so late. I say goodnight and make my way to the room I call my own while I'm here.

As tired as I am, I can't seem to fall asleep. My mind is churning and my fingers are itching to pick up my phone and call Ryker. I want to talk to him so badly.

I turned my phone off days ago when my mom kept trying to call. She knows where I am and that's all she needs to know. If I were to turn it on, would there be any messages from Ryker? Does he still have my number or did he lose it when he broke his phone?

Closing my eyes, I picture him in my mind. Thoughts of Halloween take over quickly. I'd never in my life done something so risque. Letting him touch me on the dancefloor was the start of my eventual fall.

I didn't have a clue that I was talking to him on the computer. His hacking of his best friend's account was something else altogether. I can't say I'm mad about it.

The night in the hotel was one of the most erotic of my life and we had many more of those moments in the short time we were together. Do I miss him or the way he made me feel?

These doubts keep crawling into my head and I hate them for making me doubt everything I know to be true.

Ryker doesn't seem like a person who would just tell a woman he loves them without meaning it. Knowing how he felt about his sister, there's absolutely no way he'd lie about something that important. I curl onto my side and close my eyes again. Thinking about Ryker calms me enough to sleep.

Sound sleep is a blessing most of the time. Now is not one of them. Being in the same position on a bed that isn't mine, has made me stiff and achy. I turn my phone on and the disappointment at not having any messages from Ryker surprises me.

I find Tyne's computer and get set up at the small desk in the corner of my room. I send Amelia a message requesting not to be disturbed at least for a while and I start writing. As the day progresses so does my manuscript. I send several chapters off to the editor and send an email to Jason with a ticket to come visit. I ask him to stop by my apartment and give him a list of the things I need.

I loved going shopping with the girls, but I miss my pajamas and the fuzzy socks Ryker bought me a few weeks after we started dating. Thinking about it now, I don't know that we ever actually dated. We kind of jumped right in head first and didn't look back.

I looked back. He continued looking forward. Until he decided to stop looking at all. Fuck. I don't want to think about him taking his own life. I want to remember the good times. Not the bad. I need the good to keep me centered while I finish this book that tears my heart out with each page.

A knock on the door rouses me from my work. "Come in," I call.

"Hey. You've been working for hours. Dinner is ready. Come eat." Amelia says.

"I want to finish up this chapter," I tell her.

"That will still be there after. Come. Eat." She orders while giving me a stern look. One that would put fear in the hearts of every child. But it doesn't phase me.

"I'm good."

"No, you aren't, you haven't eaten all day. Please come join us."

"Fine. I'll eat and then I'm coming right back here to write."

Amelia nods her head in agreement. I don't make it back to the book at all as we get into another game. This time: "New Phone, Who Dis?"

Ryker

I enter the office building and make my way up to the fifteenth floor. Maybe enter isn't a strong enough word. More like I storm in with the determination of a man on a mission: A mission to get back the woman I love.

Jason sits behind his sleek desk in his pressed suit taking a call which I end promptly by pulling the phone from his ear. He sits with his mouth opening and closing in surprise. Yeah, I surprised myself too.

"Let's chat, you and I."

"Ryker, right?" He finally asks.

"Where's Sydney?"

"I can't tell you that." He squirms in his seat.

"Listen up, little man. Sydney is mine. Not yours. Now tell me where she is."

"Look, man. She asked me not to tell anyone where she went. I can't break her trust."

"But I can break your jaw. Or your fingers. Which would you prefer?" I ask as I hover over him menacingly.

I won't hurt him. Not really. I just need him to believe I will. "So what's it gonna be?"

"Alright. Alright. She's in Tennessee."

"Be more specific. Tennessee is a big state."

"Fuck. She's going to kill me." He whines.

"Would you prefer I do it?"

"No. That won't be necessary. She's in Gatlinburg. I'm scheduled to take a flight to her this afternoon."

"Well, I think you won't be making that flight."

"Yeah. I see that. But you have to do something for me." I tilt my head, eyebrows raised waiting for his next words. "Take these things to her."

He gets up and walks over to a pink bag. When he brings it over, I grab the handle. He doesn't release it right away.

"For the record, nothing happened between Sydney and me. We're just friends. She still loves you so don't fuck it up." He tells me.

I look around the office. "How's it feel?"

"How does what feel?" He asks.

"Living my life."

"Lonely." He responds. "Believe it or not, you're lucky."

"Maybe. Maybe not. What do you do here anyway?"

"IT."

"We'll talk when I get back," I say and walk away. I turn back. "By the way, thanks for looking after my girl."

Jason laughs. "She can look after herself."

"No doubt. But she has some difficulty realizing that."

"I noticed. Her mom is a real piece of work. Don't change her, man."

"Never. I love her just the way she is."

Traffic is ridiculous, but I still make it to the airport in record time. I pay a huge amount of money for a last-minute flight and then fight with TSA over the size of my bag. Fearful of missing the flight, I throw my bag at them and rush through with just the clothes on my back and Sydney's belongings.

We land in Knoxville, where Sydney is supposed to be meeting Jason. I come out into the main airport and spot her immediately. There's a man with her, his arm around her shoulders.

I don't know what comes over me, but I rush him and knock him to the ground. "Don't you fucking touch her!" I scream.

The man smirks. "Ryker, I take it."

"What the hell is wrong with you?" Sydney seethes. "You mind getting off my cousin?"

Cousin? This is her cousin. The one she told me about. I stand up and then help Tyne to his feet. "Sorry about that." I apologize.

"No worries." He wipes down the front of his shirt. "If it were Amelia, I'd have done the same thing."

We shake hands. "I've heard a lot about you," I say.

"Same here. Though Sydney never mentioned a jealous streak."

"I didn't even realize I had one," I reply.

"Excuse me. Ryker, what are you doing here and why do you have my stuff?"

"I visited Jason and he told me where you were. It seemed A little much to have him fly out here with your belongings when I was headed here anyway."

"Jason told you where I was? That fucking prick."

"Now hold on, sweetheart. I didn't give him much choice in the matter."

"What did you do?" She hisses.

"Nothing, baby. Jason and I are good friends." I lie.

We aren't yet, but I'm sure we will be eventually. Tyne stands by with a smile. "Where are your bags? I'm assuming you plan to stay and this isn't just a day trip."

"My shit is back at the other airport."

"Why?" Sydney asks.

"Because it was either bring your things or mine. I chose to bring yours."

"And what will you do for clothes, walk around naked?"

"That could be fun."

"Absolutely not! No one gets to see you naked but me." She snaps.

"Ah, babe. You want to see me naked?"

At this point, we're gathering quite the crowd. I suppose tackling someone in the airport will do that. I see TSA agents coming our way. "Is everything okay here?" One of them asks.

"Sure. Sure. I just got a tad excited. I haven't been with my girl in months. You know how it is right?" I ask.

The two men look at us suspiciously. "Well, if you have your things, you should probably leave the airport."

"Absolutely, sir. We were just leaving." Tyne says. Sydney follows and pulls me along.

"Shopping first, then home?" Tyne asks us.

"No. Take me home." Sydney says. "Then you boys can go wherever you want."

"You should come with us," I say.

"I have a book to finish."

"You're writing? That's amazing!" I tell her honestly. The last time she and I seriously talked, she was struggling to finish one project and her publisher was expecting at least one more before the end of the year.

"Yeah, I am." She says. She averts her eyes from mine like she's guilty to be writing again.

I place my hand on her shoulder. "Hey. I'm proud of you."

She turns away and looks out the window. I leave her to her thoughts and following her lead, I take in the scenery. I've never had the chance to visit Tennessee and have always wanted to see this area.

It's breathtaking, but not more so than the woman sitting in front of me. I see it clearly now. She's removed all the dye from her hair and she wears no makeup, letting her natural beauty shine through. This is how I prefer her. Comfortable in her own skin rather than playing dress up for others.

Tyne's house is gorgeous. It's a full mountain cabin with rich woods and even has a porch swing. Suddenly, I can picture Sydney and I enjoying a cup of coffee as we swing and look out over the mountains.

Sydney looks back over her shoulder. "Why are you here?" She asks.

"I needed to see you. Needed to explain a few things. Then if you really, truly want me to leave, I will."

I hope she doesn't want me to leave.

Sydney

Of course, I don't want him to leave. I want him to stay forever. But I won't tell him that. I'll listen to what he has to say and then he can be on his merry way back to his life. I've made up my mind.

Have you? My mind argues. *Just look at him. You don't want him going anywhere unless it's the bedroom.* Stupid brain.

"Ryker, be serious for just a minute, please. What are you doing here?"

"Seriously, I wanted to give you something and it couldn't wait. It's in your bag. Now, go. Don't worry about me. I'm going to have Tyne take me to rent a car and then I'm going to go shopping for some clothes."

"You flew all the way here because you wanted to give me something?"

"Yes. But if you don't want me here, I'll find a hotel. I'm sure there are plenty to choose from down in the city."

He's going to be a distraction, but I can't let him pay for a room. Hotels are expensive and he's a fucking bouncer. An out-of-work one at that. "No. You can stay here. For now. Tyne has a spare bedroom down the hall. Come on and I'll show you."

I can see the disappointment in his eyes, but I'm not about to offer him my bed. Like I said he's going to be a distraction. Not only that, but I don't want him to see the book until I figure out how to tell him that the story is about him.

I lead him down the hall, show him the spare room, and head back to mine. I open my bag and pull out my laptop. I place it on the little desk and then see a manilla envelope sitting where the laptop used to be. It's heavy in my hand and I hesitate to open it.

I lay it back in my suitcase, afraid to open it. I go back and forth several times before I finally get the courage to just rip the bandaid off. Pulling it back out, I gingerly open the little metal clasp at the top. Inside is a notebook of some kind.

I pull it out and see the word *journal* written across the top. Is this what I think it is? Does Ryker want me to read this? I change into comfortable pants and a sweater and curl into the pillows on the bed. Just a few pages, and then I'll get to writing.

Hours. I spent hours reading through journal entry after journal entry. Not only did I take a deep dive into Ryker's feelings, but now I know more about his past than I ever did. I know that his father was always hard on him and his sister. His mother sat back and watched while he berated and bullied them.

I know that Stacey married a man just like her father, only worse. He didn't stop at the emotional abuse. He liked to beat up on her and seemed to get off on it. His sister was raised to be the perfect wife, so even though she went to Ryker with her issues and for help, that didn't stop her from standing by her husband in the end.

Had Ryker killed him, his sister would still be alive. He'd gladly spend the rest of his life behind bars if it meant his sister and niece were alive and well. His mother has tried to talk with him on occasion, but the conversation is always stilted and it ends up being uncomfortable for them both.

What hurts my heart the most is learning that he wasn't mad at me for running, he understood. He was disappointed because I did exactly what he expected when I ran. I did what everyone else has done. Tom has been the only constant in his life and for that I am thankful.

Ryker doesn't feel worthy of love and thinks that karma is out to get him for the mistakes he made. I don't believe in karma, and if anyone deserves love, it's him. He deserves everything.

When I get to the middle of the journal, a piece of loose paper falls out. I pick it up and open it. It's a letter. It's addressed to me.

Sydney,

If you're reading this, then you've read at least half of the journal. While I didn't write that journal for you, it was the easiest way to talk to you about my past. I don't want there to be any secrets between us.

Everything I wrote is true. My feelings have been all over the place since my sister died and you are the first thing that helped me feel grounded. I know I said that I was letting you go, but I realized while I was in Hope House that I couldn't do it.

I love you and my life has less meaning without you in it. My sister used to tell me to find someone I wanted to dream with. You know, where you dream of a future. Make sure you can see her in every snapshot of your life. That's how you'll know it's real.

She admitted to me once that she fucked up when she agreed to marry Chester. That was her husband's name. Who names their kids after the orange cat on the puffed cheese snacks? Anyway, she once told me that when she pictured her future, he wasn't the man in any of the snapshots of her life.

She chose wrong and it got her killed. It wasn't my fault. I know that now. Either way, my sister was dead. It would have been physical or emotional. I'm not sure which one, but does it really matter? It's all the same. What's the point in living if you can't feel it?

That's what scares me so much, you know. It's that you make me feel. EVERYTHING. When I look at you I see hope. When we kissed, I felt your love for me. And when you ran away, I felt fear unlike any I'd ever felt before.

Please don't make me go back to unfeeling. Please love me back.

Yours,

Ryker

Ryker

Tyne refused to let me pay for a rental. Instead, he loaned me one of his cars and then drove me into town himself. Luckily, they have a Target, because I just don't think I'm the bejeweled shirt and cowboy boots type of person.

I was going to let Sydney know I was leaving, but when I got to her door, I heard her whimpering and knew she had to be reading the journal. The one that detailed my life.

I didn't give that to her in the hopes she'd take me back out of pity. I wanted her to truly see me. To know that she and I are a lot alike in the way our pasts shaped us.

Tyne let it slip that her new book is inspired by me and that she worried I would think she was using me for the story. I like that I inspire her. Even if it is all the dirty parts that get her creative juices flowing. Now that she has that journal, she can use it too. I don't care.

Maybe she'll be open to reading the other journals. There are several. She can see them when we go home. Or I can have Tom send them down here.

Tyne has told me a little about his and Sydney's past. It's not anything I don't already know. Not because Syd told me outright but because of little things she would say: *Mom said I don't look good in flannel, Mom thinks this dress shows off too much of the fat on my sides. Mom said more is less when it comes to makeup.*

Honestly, I'm surprised sometimes by how well-rounded Sydney is. I think about telling her to write her mother into a story just to kill her off within the pages. I can think of some pretty creative ideas for how her death would go down. Maybe she can do the same for my dad and Warren.

I pick up dinner for everyone while we're out. Tyne said his fiance, cousin- a different one- and his cousin's girl would be joining us so I ordered a ton of food. "Do you really run a distillery?" I ask Tyne on our drive back to the house.

"Yeah. We specialize in moonshine. Amelia is a wine connoisseur. We've been working on merging our two family's businesses."

"That sounds seriously fascinating," I say.

"Yeah. You should come by while you're in town. I'll give you a tour."

"Sure. I'd like that."

"Sydney said you're a bouncer. You met at a bar, right?"

"Yeah. There's a little more to my career than Sydney knows."

"What? Do you own the bar?" He chuckles like he just told a joke. I could own the bar if I wanted. I could own a hundred of them.

"Nah. I actually work in security. I create apps that help companies track their assets and secure their inventory without it being noticeable. I also do home security as well."

"Nice. I've been meaning to look into something like that for the distillery. Is it mass-marketed?"

"No. I build the systems and personalize them based on the individual business needs."

"Sweet! You definitely need to come by for that tour and talk to me more about this security and IT stuff."

"Definitely," I say. "Thanks for being so understanding at the airport. I appreciate it."

"Don't mention it. Just don't hurt her again and we'll be golden."

"I never meant to hurt her in the first place," I say.

"I know that. If I thought you had, I'd have already shot you with my hunting rifle. Then I'd have thrown you from the mountainside and let the bear have you."

"How about this, if I hurt her again, I'll throw myself from the nearest cliff?"

"Don't let Sydney hear you talk like that. It worried her when she heard you'd seriously considered offing yourself."

"I know." I sigh. "I don't think I'd have actually gone through with it."

"The fact that you admitted yourself into a mental health facility proves that you would have."

I hadn't thought of that. I guess he's right. Deep down I knew I needed help and that was my outcry. Thank God Tom heard it.

Back at the house, Amelia is waiting along with two other people she introduces as Carrie and Chad. I sit the food on the counter and turn to shake hands with everyone. "Are you a football player?" Amelia asks.

"No?" I ask instead of stating because I'm confused.

"Oh. I just figured since you tackled my fiance in the middle of the airport that maybe you were."

"Sorry about that," I say sincerely. "My jealousy got the best of me for a minute."

"I'm just fucking with you. But please refrain from damaging him. I don't want him in a cast on our wedding day."

"Please. The only reason you care is because you want all the attention on your special day." Carrie pipes up.

"Is that so bad?" Amelia asks. "It is my day after all."

"No. It's your and Tyne's day." Carries replies.

"Nah. It's her day. All I have to do is show up." Tyne cuts in.

"I promise not to hurt him," I interject before they can continue arguing over the wedding.

"That's all I ask," Amelia says squeezing my arm. "Now can we eat? I'm starving."

"You guys go ahead. I'm going to go grab Sydney." I say and head down the hall.

There's no light coming from under the door, so I quietly open it and step in. Sydney is curled up on the bed fast asleep with my journal in her hands. Her computer emits a blue glow and I walk over to it. I don't mean to snoop, but I've been dying to know what she's writing.

A few months ago, it would have been the first thing she told me, but even that has changed. I begin to read and it doesn't take long to notice that her book is familiar. The male in her story sounds an awful lot like me. I continue reading, in awe of the words she's written. This is my story.

It's my life she's writing within those pages. Not a replica, but enough for me to notice. She's portrayed me as a vulnerable male and my female counterpart as a strong, independent woman. As if she's trying to reverse our roles.

Suddenly, a light comes on behind me, and the computer is slammed closed. "I'm sorry," Sydney states. "I swear I was going to tell you."

"Tell me what? That you were writing about me?"

"Yes." She says. "You don't seem mad." She sounds surprised.

"Because I'm not. I'm honored." I say.

"You are?"

"Yeah. I'm alright being your muse, so long as you're writing again." I know how much she struggled to get the last book out and how disappointed she was in it.

Her shoulders drop in relief. "I thought you'd be upset."

"Never. Plus, Stacey deserves to have her story told. Even if no one knows it's her."

Sydney stands there for several minutes before saying anything. I start to get worried when she just stares at me. "I read your journal. At least part of it. Thank you for sharing it with me."

"I owed it to you. I'm sorry I didn't tell you everything from the beginning."

"I understand why you didn't. I'm sorry I ran away."

I shrug. "Can we start over?"

She shakes her head. "No. Starting over isn't possible." I deflate. It's fine. I'll be fine. "But, we can move on from here." She offers.

"I'd like that," I tell her.

I don't know who moves first, but we quickly close the space between us. She jumps and I catch her under her thighs. Our lips crash together so hard, I taste blood in my mouth and feel a sharp pain when teeth have split the skin. Sydney swipes her tongue out and licks the blood away.

My dick goes hard in an instant. "That's so fucking hot." I hiss, my voice low and husky. Then I prove to her just how hot by grinding her down on the bulge inside my pants.

Now she's the one hissing while I moan. "Off." She pants while jerking on my shirt. I let her go just long enough to remove the shirt from my body and then I lift her back up again. She begins to kiss down my neck and across the part of my chest she can reach.

"Get on the bed," I order placing her back on her feet again.

She starts to back away and I twist to turn on the lamp and turn off the bright overhead light. Her hands are back on me, but the touch is different. Reverant as she takes in the tattoo that now takes up the space on my back.

Her fingers trace the lines of the tattoo. "When did you get this?"

"Right after I was discharged from Hope House."

"It's beautiful." She says awestruck. It is. The tattoo artist did an amazing job. "Is that me?"

I nod. "From the first night we met."

The tattoo is an angel, well the back of one. With flowing brown-blonde hair and grey wings that span both shoulders. "You are my angel, Syd. Even if you never realized it." I whisper.

I twist back around to face her and see tears in her eyes. Before they can fall, I grab her chin. "Do you remember what I told you that night?"

When she tilts her head in thought, I fill in the blanks. "Your friend said you should lick me and I said I was down for that, but if you did I got to lick you back. I said that I'd likely bite you but that wouldn't be enough. I'd devour you."

"I remember." She says huskily.

"I am a man of my word, so get on the bed," I order one more time.

She rushes to follow my directions, flinging her clothes across the room with no care as to where they land. Once she's positioned with her head lying on the pillow and her legs spread, I saunter over like I have all the time in the world.

She squirms under my attention, but I love that she doesn't move to cover herself. Her belly is soft and will one day make the perfect home for a growing child. Her hips are a little thicker, but they're perfect to hold on to and that ass. Damn, that ass. The way it jiggles when I fuck her from behind is every man's wet dream.

I just stand at the foot of the bed taking her in. She rubs her thighs together and they come apart slick with her arousal. "I'm going to go down on you until you can't talk for all the screaming you'll do," I warn.

Her eyes light up at the words. She wants this. "You're going to be a good girl and wrap those thighs around my head aren't you?"

"Yes." She moans."

"I want to feel them squeeze me when you come." I don't give her a chance to respond because I can't hold back anymore. I need to taste her.

There's no sweet workup, no smooth circle of my fingers along her folds and clit. Oh, no. I take my bite and she screams. That sound is music to my ears, a sound I have only been able to dream about in the months we've been apart.

I punish her for that absence by making her sing. Her body responds to me as if trained and I work her as if that's true. I don't think I'll ever get enough of her taste, but my dick is so hard it hurts and it needs the relief of her hot, wet pussy. I kiss her stomach and then her breasts before lining myself up and thrusting home.

If anyone ever told me connecting to a woman, body to body, would feel like I had come home, I'd have laughed in their face. Now,

I understand. This is what men and women wait a lifetime for. This connection. Because it's not just a connection of the body. It's the connection of two souls.

It's been too damn long since I've felt like this. I still don't think I deserve this happiness, but in this, I'm going to be selfish. I'm taking this happiness and I'm never letting it go.

Sydney

I fell asleep wrapped up in Ryker's arms, warm and safe. How is it that this man, one who is a convicted felon and has more issues than Seventeen Magazine, is my safety? I can't answer that question, but I don't think I need to. I need to just accept it.

"You hungry?" Ryker asks me as he kisses the back of my neck. "I was supposed to be coming in here to get you for dinner."

"That was hours ago," I say, giggling. I roll over so that I can look at him.

"Sorry, not sorry." He says, shrugging one shoulder, a shit-eating grin on his face. "I was hungry for something else."

"Can we talk about the journal?" I ask.

While he doesn't look thrilled with the idea, he agrees. We dress and sneak into the kitchen. I say sneak because we try our best not to make too much noise and wake anyone. After Ryker has filled two plates with food and grabbed both drinks, we go back to my room.

While we eat, we talk. He tells me more about his past. I tell him about mine. I'm flabbergasted when he tells me that he lives in a penthouse apartment in Manhattan and owns his own security IT firm. He moonlights as a bouncer because it allows him to, in some way, protect others.

He laughs when I tell him stories of getting locked in one of the big metal vats at the distillery when I was a kid. He threatens to hurt my mother for her passive-aggressive comments about my looks. I tell him she's most definitely not worth serving any more time behind bars.

By the time we're done talking, I feel like I know him so much better, and the more I learn, the more I love him. I think he feels the same.

Just before sunrise, I pull Ryker out of the house and up the trail that leads to Tyne's private overlook. I have a thermos of coffee and a blanket. When we reach the top, I lay the blanket out and sit down. Ryker sits beside me.

"Wow!" He exclaims. "I now understand why they call them the Smokey Mountains."

"Yeah. You can see it so clearly right before dawn. It's one of my favorite things about this place."

"Yeah? What are the others?"

"The quiet. It allows me to think, you know. In the city, there's always so much noise that my thoughts sometimes get lost in it."

"I get that. I remember when I was a kid thinking how amazing it would be to live in the city. Then when I got older, all I wanted was to get as far away from New York as possible."

"Is that why you joined the Army?"

"Partly. It was also a good way to rebel against what my father expected of me."

"I swear when we have kids, I am not going to force them into any life. They will get to choose where their life takes them." I say, vehemently.

"We?" Ryker asks and I go back over what I just said. Oh, shit. "Don't look so scared. I like the sound of we." He tells me.

"Isn't it too soon?" I ask.

"To talk about a life together? I don't think so. I love you and I suspect you love me. Plus, who makes the rules? No one gets to tell us how we feel or what's a good time to start talking about things."

"I like the way you think. And yes, I love you, Ryker."

He leans in and kisses me. I shiver. "Let's get back. You're cold."

"I'm not," I argue. "But if you're so concerned, you could hold me and keep me warm."

He does. He pulls me in between his legs and wraps me up in his arms. We sit on the top of the mountain until the sun fully rises.

We get back to the house just as Tyne sets plates on the table. He doesn't say anything about us missing dinner the night before, but he does give me a look that lets me know he heard everything going on in my bedroom. He's never been one to judge. When he sees my hand entwined with Ryker's he offers me a smile.

Tyne just gets me. He's more like a crazy big brother than a cousin and the only thing he would ever want is for me to be happy. He would kill for me if needed, and vice versa. That helps me understand more where Ryker's mind was when he went after Stacey's husband. He didn't do anything wrong in my eyes.

"Do you two have plans for today?" Tyne asks. "I was going to take Ryker on a tour of the distillery."

"That sounds fun. Can I come?"

"Absolutely. The more the merrier." He responds.

I wiggle in my seat. I have been dying to see what changes he's made to the place. "Just let me shower and we can go."

As I walk away, I can hear him laugh under his breath and say, "Yeah. Do that. You smell like sex."

Christmas Eve

The last few months have been a whirlwind. I released my newest book and to my utter surprise and pleasure, it is an international bestseller. Ryker and I came back from Tennessee a few days after our reconciliation and things are good. They're really good.

I met with my mother a few days ago and let her know that I would not be coming to the annual Christmas party. She argued how important it was to Warren and I told her that Ryler was more important. I also gave her a little insight into the man she married.

She scoffed and complained that Ryker was lying. I told her that he actually wasn't and that I had proof if she ever wanted to see it. She changed the subject and began to talk about my weight, she's pissed I took all the blonde out of my hair, because how dare I look like my father.

I told her in no uncertain terms that so long as she felt the need to put me down, I would not talk to her. I also let her know that Warren wasn't welcome anywhere near me or Ryker.

Ryker has been speaking to his mom more. I think she's trying to bridge the divide. She's a really sweet woman, she's just been stuck for so long in a marriage with a man who doesn't appreciate a woman's opinion, that she expects all men to be the same.

I feel sorry for her. It doesn't excuse her not defending her children, but it has helped Ryker to understand. As for his father, that man can rot in Hell. He about had a heart attack when he discovered that his only son, who he disowned, was in charge of all the security in his firm.

He demanded all the monies that had been paid to Ryker be returned. We had to remind him that there was a binding contract and that the lawyers would have a field day with him if he even tried.

Ryker has handed me a journal on the first day of every month for me to read. Once I'm done, he sits and lets me ask any questions I have and he answers them all. I reread the letters he wrote to me often. Just seeing the words he took the time to put down on paper, gives me so much hope for the future. He doesn't like to talk about things a lot. He'd prefer to handle it all internally, but he's working on it. The journals and the letters are part of that.

My man is a work in progress, but at least he's willing to do the work. He acknowledges his flaws and he's teaching me that it's okay to have my own. "Baby, come open one of your presents." He calls from the living room of his penthouse apartment.

He's tried several times to get me to move in, but I keep refusing. I like having my own space. Plus, my office is set up at my place. That's where all my work is done. "Coming," I call, placing the last dish in the dishwasher.

I step into the living room and he stands there with a long slim box in his hands. He hands it over and I rip the bow off. Inside is what looks like another journal. "What is this?" I ask because the outside isn't labeled like the others he's let me read.

"Open it." He says.

I pull back the front cover and see my name on the first page. When I look up again, Ryker is in front of me kneeling on a bent knee with a small box in his hands. "Sydney, up until recently I thought that I was unloveable. I thought my sister died hating me. But I've realized that she doesn't hate me because she sent me you.

There's no other person on this earth or beyond that would ever find me worthy of being loved by you."

"I understand now that it wasn't my strength that kept me from pulling the trigger that night. It was yours. It was your voice in my head telling me not to give up. Letting me know that there was always a rainbow after the storm."

"Baby, I'm sure we'll face many storms in our lives, but I want to be the rainbow for you. I want to be the good parts of your life that outweigh the bad. Will you marry me?"

Tears fall from my eyes blurring my vision, but I don't need to see to know that Ryker has a small but hesitant smile on his face. I know that his eyes are shining with a love so deep it puts any romance novel to shame. This man, the one that I love with my whole heart is on bended knee asking me to marry him, and I'm standing here saying nothing.

"Yes." I finally blurt, my throat tight with emotion. "Yes, I'll marry you."

He pulls the ring out of the box and slides it onto my finger. He stands and kisses me softly.

"I know I'm not a perfect man, but I am the perfect man for you. I love you."

"I love you too," I say, admiring my ring.

"What did you wish for this year?" He asks.

"For you. I wished for you." I tell him.

"Then it's an honor to make that wish and all the wishes for the rest of your life come true."

I sit on the sofa admiring the journal still in my hands. I flip the pages and see both letters that Ryker wrote to me. Both letters are at two different times in his life. The first was a letter filled with regret and a resignation that still hurts to read. The second, while equally emotional, is more lighthearted than the first. It was when he made up his mind to fight for me. For us.

I read over them now. Just snippets that I highlighted because they stuck out to me.

At another time, in another place, we could have been great. Hell, we were great for a short while. Don't let your mom or anyone else dictate your life okay? Promise me. Be undeniably you, always. Because everything you are is beautiful.

The only time I'm comfortable in my own skin is when I'm with Ryker. That's when I can be undeniably me. He gives me the courage to be me.

My sister used to tell me to find someone I wanted to dream with. You know, where you dream of a future. Make sure you can see her in every snapshot of your life. That's how you'll know it's real.

When I close my eyes it's Ryker I see sharing a future with. I can picture the family we'll have, the trips we'll take, and the life we'll build together. I can't wait to get started.

That's what scares me so much, you know. It's that you make me feel. EVERYTHING. When I look at you I see hope. When we kissed, I felt your love for me. And when you ran away, I felt fear unlike any I'd ever felt before. Don't let me go back to unfeeling. Please love me back.

Ryker makes me feel too. And I love every bit of it. The confidence I feel every time he tells me I'm beautiful. The love I feel when I look at him. The hope he gives me when he talks about what kind of life he wants us to have.

For a man who claims not to be able to talk about things, he has a way with words. My vision blurs, tears gathering at the edges of my eyes. I thought the crying was over. I swipe the tears away as words fill my head. I rush to the computer and begin to write. This is a new story. One yet to be written........

Last Christmas I wished for a date to my family holiday party. Falling in love wasn't on my bingo card, but here I am, loving a man who didn't think he was deserving. Here we are together, after one hell of a set of storms. And now, we can finally see the rainbow.

Also by Angie Cottingham

<u>Paranormal Romance</u>
The Weaver Chronicles: Reegan
Make a Wish
The Lady Of Nightmares
<u>Contemporary Small Town Romance</u>
Once Upon a New Year
<u>Dark Contemporary</u>
Wild Ring (Book 1 in the Wild Duet)
Wild Rules (Book 2 in the Wild Duet
<u>Dark Mafia Romance</u>
Prince of Chaos

The Mafia King's Obsession (Prequal to the Devil's of Lands End)

Coming Soon

Fade: The Lost Blood Fae Queen (TBD)

Tempted by The Devils: The Devils of Land's End (TBD)

Addicted to the Pain (The Devil's of Land's End (TBD)

Wild Ride: A Wild Duet spin-off (TBD)

Wild Nights: A Wild Duet spin-off (TBD)

All dates are subject to change.

Milton Keynes UK
Ingram Content Group UK Ltd.
UKHW030855111124
451035UK00001B/46